No one writes romantic fiction like Barbara Cartland.

Miss Cartland was originally inspired by the best of the romantic novelists she read as a girl—writers such as Elinor Glyn, Ethel M. Dell and E. M. Hull. Convinced that her own wide audience would also delight in her favorite authors, Barbara Cartland has taken their classic tales of romance and specially adapted them for today's readers.

Bantam is proud to publish these novels—personally selected and edited by Miss Cartland—under the imprint

BARBARA CARTLAND'S
LIBRARY OF LOVE

Bantam books by Barbara Cartland
Ask your bookseller for the books you have missed

The Money Moon

by Jeffrey Farnol

Condensed by Barbara Cartland

BANTAM BOOKS · TORONTO · NEW YORK · LONDON

THE MONEY MOON
A Bantam Book / August 1979

ISBN 0–553–12616–4

Published simultaneously in the United States and Canada

Bantam Books are published by Bantam Books, Inc. Its trade-
mark, consisting of the words "Bantam Books" and the por-
trayal of a bantam, is Registered in U.S. Patent and Trademark
Office and in other countries. Marca Registrada. Bantam
Books, Inc., 666 Fifth Avenue, New York, New York 10019.

PRINTED IN THE UNITED STATES OF AMERICA

Introduction
by
Barbara Cartland

This is one of the novels I read when I was very young, and it made me believe in real romance and in a love that was strong, yet tender, passionate, and kind.

I wanted to grow up to be as kind, sweet, and proud as Anthea and to find a husband as gentle, determined, and possessive as George, the disillusioned millionaire.

"...," he was beginning, but 'An—
interrupted him.
"...ar, don't Prudence send you to

Chapter
One

When Sylvia Marchmont went to Europe
(adequately chaperoned, of course), George Bellew, being at the same time desirous of testing his
most recently acquired yacht, followed her, and
mutual friends in New York, Newport, and
elsewhere confidently awaited news of their engagement.

Great, therefore, was their surprise when they
learnt of her approaching marriage to the Duke of
Ryde.

Bellew, being young and rich, had many
friends (a quite natural result), who, while they
sympathised with his loss, yet agreed amongst
themselves, and with great unanimity, that despite
Bellew's millions, Sylvia had done vastly well for
herself, seeing that a Duke is always a Duke, especially in America.

When Bellew heard of her engagement he
rang for Baxter, his valet.

Baxter had been his father's valet before him,
and as to age might have been thirty, or forty, or
fifty, as he stood there beside the table, with one

1

eyebrow raised a trifle higher than the other, waiting for Bellew to speak.

"Baxter."

"Sir?"

"Take a seat."

"Thank you, Sir."

"Baxter, I wish to consult with you."

"As between master and servant, Sir?"

"As between man and man, Baxter."

"Very good, Mr. George, Sir."

"I should like to hear your opinion, Baxter, as to what is the proper and most accredited course to adopt when one has been—er—crossed in love."

"Excuse me, Mr. George, but am I to understand you as meaning heart-broke, as it were, or merely—jilted?"

"What is the difference?"

"A great deal, Sir."

"Then let us say—both, Baxter."

"Well then, Sir," began Baxter, slightly wrinkling his smooth brow, "so far as I can call to mind, the courses usually adopted by despairing lovers are, in number, four—though there are doubtless numerous others."

"Name them, Baxter."

"First, Mr. George, there is what I may term the course Retaliatory—which is marriage . . ."

"Marriage?"

"With another party, Sir, on the principle that there are as good fish in the sea as ever came out, and—er—pebbles on beaches, Sir. You understand me, Sir?"

"Perfectly, go on."

"Secondly, there is the Army, Sir; I have

known of a good many enlistments on account of blighted affections, Mr. George, Sir. Indeed, the Army is very popular."

"Ah?" Bellew replied, settling the tobacco in his pipe with the aid of a self-spoon. "Proceed, Baxter."

"Thirdly, Mr. George, there are those who are content to merely disappear."

"Hm."

"And lastly, Sir, though it is usually the first, there is dissipation, Mr. George. Drink, Sir —the consolation of bottles and . . ."

"Exactly!" Bellew nodded. "Now, Baxter, knowing me as you do, what course should you advise me to adopt?"

"You mean, Mr. George, speaking as between man and man, of course—you mean that you are in the unfortunate position of being crossed in your affections, Sir?"

"Also broken-hearted, Baxter."

"Certainly, Sir!"

"Miss Marchmont marries the Duke of Ryde in three weeks, Baxter."

"Indeed, Sir!"

"You were, I believe, aware of the fact that Miss Marchmont and I were as good as engaged?"

"I had—hem!—gathered as much, Sir."

"Then confound it all, Baxter, why aren't you surprised?"

"I am quite overcome, Sir," Baxter replied.

"Consequently," pursued Bellew, "I am—er—broken-hearted, Baxter."

"Certainly, Sir."

"Crushed, despondent, and utterly hopeless,

Baxter, and shall be, henceforth, pursued by the
—er—Haunting Spectre of the Might Have Been."

"Very natural, Sir, indeed!"

"I could have hoped, Baxter, that, having
served me so long, not to mention my father, you
would have shown just a—er—shade more feeling
in the matter."

"And if you were to ask me—as between man
and man, Sir—why I don't show more feeling than
speaking as the old servant of your respected
father, Master George, Sir—I should beg most respectfully to say that regarding the lady in question, her conduct is not in the least surprising,
Miss Marchmont, being a beauty, Master George,
and therefore vain, spoilt, and shallow.

"Referring to your heart, Sir, I am ready to
swear that it is not even cracked! And now, Sir—
what clothes do you propose to wear this morning?"

"And pray, why should you be so confident
regarding the condition of my heart?"

"Because, Sir, speaking as your father's old
servant, Master George, I make bold to say that
I don't believe that you have ever been in love, or
even know what love is, Sir."

"Nevertheless," Bellew answered, shaking his
head, "I can see for myself the dreary perspective
of a hopeless future, Baxter, blasted by the
Haunted Spectre of the Might Have Been; I'll trouble you to push the cigarettes a little nearer."

"And now, Sir," Baxter said, as he rose to strike
and apply the necessary match, "what suit will
you wear today?"

"Something in tweeds."

"Tweeds, Sir! Surely you forget your appoint-
ment with the Lady Cecily Prynne and her party?

Lord Mount-clair had me on the telephone last night..."

"Also a good heavy walking-stick, Baxter, and a knapsack."

"A knapsack, Sir?"

"I shall set out on a walking-tour—in an hour's time."

"Certainly, Sir—where to, Sir?"

"I haven't the least idea, Baxter, but I'm going in an hour. On the whole, of the four courses you describe for one whose life is blighted, whose heart—I say, whose heart, Baxter, is broken—utterly smashed, and—er—shattered beyond repair, I prefer to disappear in an hour, Baxter."

"Shall you drive the touring-car, Sir, or the new racer?"

"I shall walk, Baxter, alone, in an hour."

* * *

It was upon a certain August morning that George Bellew shook the dust of London from his feet, leaving Chance, or Destiny, to direct him.

Thus it was that, being careless of his ultimate destination, Fortune condescended to take him under her wing (if she has one), and guided his steps across the river into the lovely land of Kent, which has been called, and very rightly, the Garden of England.

He began very well (for Bellew); in the morning he walked very nearly five miles, and in the afternoon, before he discovered it, he accomplished ten more, on a hay-cart that happened to be going in his direction.

He had swung himself up amongst the hay, unobserved by the somnolent driver, and had

ridden thus an hour or more, in that delicious state
between waking and sleeping, before the Waggoner discovered him.

The Waggoner ordered him from the cart,
and he slowly descended.

No sooner was he fairly on the road than the
Waggoner went for him with a rush and a whirl of
knotted fists. It was very dusty in that particular
spot, so that it presently rose in a cloud, in the
midst of which the battle raged, fast and furious.

And in a while the Waggoner, rising out of the
ditch, grinned to see Bellew wiping the blood
from his face.

"You be no fool!" said the Waggoner, panting.

"Thank you," replied Bellew, "though there
are others who think differently, I believe."

"Leastways, not wi' your fists," said the Waggoner, mopping his face with the end of his neck-
cloth.

"Why, you are pretty good yourself, if it
comes to that," returned Bellew, mopping in his
turn.

Thus they stood awhile, stanching their
wounds, and gazing upon each other with a mutual and growing respect.

"Well," enquired Bellew, when he had re-
covered his breath somewhat, "shall we begin
again, or do you think we have had enough? To
be sure, I begin to feel much better for your efforts.

"You see, exercise is what I most need just
now, on account of the—er—Haunting Spectre of
the Might Have Been, to offset its effect, you
know; but it is uncomfortably warm work here in
the sun, isn't it?"

"Ah," the Waggoner nodded, "it be."

"Then suppose we—er—continue our journey?" said Bellew, with his dreamy gaze upon the tempting load of sweet-smelling hay.

"Ah!" The Waggoner nodded again, beginning to roll down his sleeves. "Suppose we do; I aren't above giving a lift to a chap as can use 'is fists—not even if 'e is a vagrant, and a uncommon dusty one at that, so, if you're in the same mind about it, up you get."

"Friend," Bellew asked, as the waggon creaked upon its way, "do you smoke?"

"Ah." The Waggoner nodded.

"Then here are three cigars which you didn't manage to smash just now."

"Cigars! Why, it ain't often as I gets so far as a cigar, unless it be squire, or parson—cigars, eh?"

Saying which, he turned and accepted the cigars, which he proceeded to stow away in the cavernous interior of his wide-eaved hat, handling them with elaborate care, rather as if they were explosives of a highly dangerous kind.

Meanwhile, George Bellew, American citizen and millionaire, lay upon the broad of his back, staring up at the cloudless blue above, and, despite heartbreak and a certain "haunting shadow," felt singularly content, which feeling he was at some pains with himself to account for.

"It must be the exercise," he said, speaking his thought aloud, as he stretched luxuriously upon his soft and fragrant couch; "after all, there is nothing like a little exercise."

"That's what they all say," the Waggoner nodded; "but I notice as them as says it ain't over-fond o' doing it—they mostly prefer to lie on their backs an' talk about it—like yourself."

"Hm. 'Some are born to exercise, some achieve exercise, and some, like myself, have exercise thrust upon them.' But anyway, it is a very excellent thing, more especially if one is affected with a—er—broken heart."

"A wot?" enquired the Waggoner.

"Blighted affections, then." Bellew sighed, settling himself more comfortably in the hay.

"You aren't 'inting at love, are you?" enquired the Waggoner, cocking a somewhat sheepish eye at him.

"I was, but, just at present ..." Bellew lowered his voice, "it is a—er—rather painful subject with me; let us, therefore, talk of something else."

"You don't mean to say that your 'eart's broke, do ye?" enquired the Waggoner, in a tone of such vast surprise and disbelief that Bellew turned and indignantly propped himself on an elbow.

"And why the deuce not?" he retorted. "My heart is no more impervious than anyone else's, confound it!"

"But," the Waggoner went on, "you ain't got the look of a 'eart-broke cove, no more than Squire Cassilis, which the same I heard telling Miss Anthea as 'is 'eart were broke, no later than yesterday, at two o'clock in the arternoon, as ever was."

"Anthea," repeated Bellew, blinking drowsily up at the sky again, "that is a very quaint name, and very pretty."

"Pretty—ah—an' so's Miss Anthea—as a pic-'ter."

"Oh, really?" asked Bellew, yawning.

"Ah," the Waggoner nodded, "there ain't a

man in or out o' the parish, from Squire down, as don't think the very same."

Here the Waggoner's voice tailed off into a meaningless drone that became merged with the creaking of the wheels and the plodding hoof-strokes of the horses, and Bellew fell asleep.

He was awakened by feeling himself shaken lustily, and, sitting up, he saw that they had come to where a narrow lane branched off from the high-road and wound away between great trees.

"Yon's your way." The Waggoner nodded, pointing along the high-road. "Dapplemere Village lies over yonder, 'bout a mile."

"Thank you very much," replied Bellew, "but I don't want the village."

"No?" enquired the Waggoner, scratching his head.

"Certainly not," answered Bellew.

"Then what do ye want?"

"Oh, well, I'll just go on lying here, and see what turns up—so drive on, like the good fellow you are."

"Can't be done," said the Waggoner.

"No?"

"Not nohow."

"And why not?"

"Why, since you ax me—because I don't have to drive no further. There be the farm-house, over the upland yonder—you can't see it because o' the trees, but there it be."

So Bellew sighed resignedly and climbed down into the road.

"What do I owe you?" he enquired.

"Owe me?" said the Waggoner, staring.

"For the ride, and the—er—very necessary exercise you afforded me."

"Lord," cried the Waggoner, with a sudden, great laugh, "you don't owe me nothin' for that —not nohow—I owe you one for a-knocking me into that ditch back yonder; though to be sure, I did give ye one or two good 'uns, didn't I?"

"You certainly did," Bellew answered, smiling, as he held out his hand.

"Hey, what be this?" cried the Waggoner, staring down at the bright five-shilling piece in his palm.

"Well, I rather think it's five shillings." Bellew smiled. "It's big enough, Heaven knows. English money is all okay, I suppose, but it's confoundedly confusing and rather heavy to drag around if you happen to have enough of it . . ."

"Ah," the Waggoner nodded, "but then nobody ever has enough of it—leastways, I never knowed nobody as had. Good-bye, Sir, and thankee, and good luck."

Bellew strolled along the road, breathing an air fragrant with honeysuckle from the hedges, and full of the song of the birds, pausing now and then to listen to the blythe carol of a skylark or the rich, sweet notes of a blackbird, and feeling that it was indeed good to be alive.

What with all this, the springy turf beneath his feet, and the blue expanse overhead, he began to whistle for the very joy of it, until, remembering the Haunting Spectre of the Might Have Been, he checked himself, and sighed instead.

Presently, turning from the road, he climbed a stile, and followed a narrow path that led across the meadows, and as he went, there met him a gentle wind laden with the sweet, warm scent of ripening hops and fruit.

On he went, heedless of his direction, until the sun grew low and he grew hungry. Looking about, he presently espied a nook, sheltered from the sun's level rays by a steep bank where flowers bloomed and ferns grew.

Here he sat down, unslinging his knapsack; and here it was, also, that he first encountered Small Porges.

The meeting of George Bellew and Small Porges (as he afterwards came to be called) was sudden, precipitate, and wholly unexpected.

Bellew had taken from his knapsack cheese, clasp-knife, and a crusty loaf of bread, when suddenly he was aware of a crash in the hedge above, and then of something that hurtled past him, all arms and legs; it rolled over two or three times, and eventually brought up in a sitting posture.

Lifting a lazy head, Bellew observed that it was a boy.

He was a very diminutive boy, with a round head covered with coppery curls; a boy who stared at Bellew out of a pair of very round, blue eyes, while he tenderly cherished a knee, and an elbow.

He had been on the brink of tears for a moment, but, meeting Bellew's quizzical gaze, he manfully repressed the weakness, and, lifting the small and somewhat weather-beaten cap that found a precarious perch at the back of his curly head, he gravely wished Bellew "Good-afternoon."

"Well met, my Lord Chesterfield," said Bellew, returning the salute. "Are you hurt?"

"Just a bit—on the elbow; but my name's George."

"Why—so is mine!" replied Bellew.

"Though they call me 'Georgy Porgy.'"

"Of couse they do," Bellow nodded, "they used to call me the same, once upon a time . . ."

Bellew sighed and hacked a piece from the loaf with his clasp-knife.

"Are you hungry, Georgy Porgy?"

"Yes, I am."

"Then here is bread, and cheese, and bottled stout—so, fall to, good comrade."

"Thank you, but I've got a piece of bread an' jam in my bundle."

"Bundle?"

"I dropped it as I came through the hedge; I'll get it."

As he spoke, he turned, and climbed up the bank, and presently he came back with a very small bundle that dangled from the end of a very long stick. Seating himself beside Bellew, he proceeded to open it.

"And pray," enquired Bellew, after they had munched silently together for some while, "pray, where might you be going?"

"I don't know yet," answered Georgy Porgy, with a shake of his curls.

"Good again!" exclaimed Bellew. "Neither do I."

"Though I've been thinking of Africa," continued his diminutive companion, turning the remains of the bread and jam over and over thoughtfully.

"Africa!" repeated Bellew, staring. "That's quite a goodish step from here."

"Yes," Georgy Porgy sighed; "but, you see, there's gold there, oh, lots of it. They dig it out of the ground with shovels, you know. Old Adam told me all 'bout it; an' it's gold I'm looking for —you see, I'm trying to find a fortune."

"I—er—beg your pardon," Bellew said.

"Money, you know," explained Georgy Porgy, with a patient sigh, "pounds, an' shillings, an' bank-notes in a sack, if I can get them."

"And what does such a very small Georgy Porgy want so much money for?"

"Well, it's for my Auntie, you know, so she won't have to sell her house an' go away from Dapplemere. She was telling me last night when I was in bed—she always comes to tuck me up, you know—an' she told me she was 'fraid we'd have to sell Dapplemere an' go to live somewhere else.

"I asked why, 'cause I'm fond of Dapplemere, an' so is she, an' she said 'cause she hadn't any money, an', 'Oh, Georgy,' she said, 'oh, Georgy, if we could only find enough money to pay off the ... the—' "

"Mortgage?" suggested Bellew, at a venture.

"Yes, that's it; but how did you know?"

"Never mind how, go on with your tale, Georgy Porgy."

" 'If we could only find enough money, or somebody leave us a fortune,' she said—an' she was crying too, 'cause I felt a tear fall on me, you know.

"So this morning I got up awful early, an' made myself a bundle on a stick—like Dick Whittington had when he left home—an' I started off to find a fortune."

"I see," said Bellew, nodding.

"But I haven't found anything yet," Georgy Porgy went on, with a long sigh. "I suppose money takes a lot of looking for, doesn't it?"

"Sometimes," Bellew answered. "And do you live alone with your Auntie then, Georgy Porgy?"

"Yes. Most boys live with their mothers, but that's where I'm different; I don't need one 'cause I've got my Auntie Anthea."

"Anthea," repeated Bellew, thoughtfully.

"Please," Georgy Porgy asked, with a sudden diffidence of manner, "where do you live?"

"Live," repeated Bellew, smiling, "under my hat—here, there, and everywhere, which means —nowhere in particular."

"But I—I mean—where is your home?"

"My home," replied Bellew, exhaling a great cloud of smoke, "my home lies beyond the 'bounding billow.' "

"That sounds an awful long way off."

"It is an awful long way off."

"An' where do you sleep while—while you're here?"

"Anywhere they'll let me. Tonight I shall sleep at some Inn, I suppose, if I can find one, but if not—under a hedge, or hay-rick."

"Oh, haven't you got any home of your own, then, here?"

"No."

"And you're not going home just yet, I mean across the 'bounding billow'?"

"Not yet."

"Then—please . . ."

The small boy's voice was suddenly tremulous and eager, and he laid a little grimy hand upon Bellew's sleeve.

"Please—if it isn't too much trouble—would you mind coming with me—to—to help me to find the fortune? You see, you are so very big, an' —oh, will you please?"

George Bellew sat up suddenly and smiled.

"Georgy Porgy, you can just bet your small life I will—and there's my hand on it, old chap."

Bellew's lips were solemn now, but all the best of his smile seemed, somehow, to have got into his grey eyes. So the big hand clasped the small one, and as they looked at each other there sprang up a certain understanding that was to be a bond between them which was to endure.

And thus was the compact made!

"I think," said Bellew, as he lay and puffed at his pipe again, "I think I'll call you Porges—it's shorter, easier, and, I think, altogether apt; I'll be Big Porges, and you shall be Small Porges—what do you say?"

"Yes, it's a lot better than Georgy Porgy," said the boy, nodding.

"But," he said, after a thoughtful pause, "I think, if you don't mind, I'd rather call you Uncle Porges."

"Just as you like, Porges." Bellew nodded lazily. "Have it your own way."

"You see, Dick Benney—the blacksmith's boy —has three Uncles, an' I've only got a single Aunt, so if you don't mind . . ."

"Uncle Porges it shall be, now and forever!" murmured Bellew.

"An' when d'you s'pose we'd better start?" enquired Small Porges, beginning to retie his bundle.

"Start where, nephew?"

"To find the fortune."

"Hum!" said Bellew.

"If we could manage to find some—even if it was only a very little—it would cheer her up so."

"To be sure it would," said Bellew, and, sit-

ting up, he pitched loaf, cheese, and clasp-knife
back into the knapsack, fastened it, slung it upon
his shoulders, rose, and took up his stick.

"Come on, my Porges," he said, "and whatever you do, keep your weather eye on your Uncle."

"Where d'you s'pose we'd better look first?"
enquired the Small Porges, eagerly.

"Why, first I think we'd better find your
Auntie Anthea."

"But . . ." began Porges, his face falling.

"No buts, my Porges," said Bellew, smiling as
he lay his hand upon his new-found nephew's
shoulder, "and as I said before, just keep your
eye on your Uncle."

So they set out together, Big Porges and
Small Porges, walking side by side over sun-
kissed field and meadow.

From the boy's eager lips Bellew heard much
of "Auntie Anthea," and learnt, little by little,
something of the brave fight she had made, lonely
and unaided, and burdened with ancient debt, to
make the farm of Dapplemere pay.

Likewise, Small Porges spoke learnedly of the
condition of the markets and of the distressing fall
in prices in regard to hay and wheat.

"Old Adam—he's our man, you know—he
says that farming isn't what it was in his young
days, 'specially if you happen to be a woman,
like my Auntie Anthea, an' he told me yesterday
that if he were Auntie, he'd give up trying, an'
take Mr. Cassilis at his word."

"Cassilis? Ah! And who is Mr. Cassilis?"

"He lives at Brampton Court—a great big
house 'bout a mile from Dapplemere; an' he's al-

ways asking my Auntie to marry him. But of course she won't, you know."

"Why not?"

"Well, I think it's 'cause he's got such big white teeth when he smiles—an' he's always smiling, you know."

As they trudged along together, Small Porges, with one hand clasped in Bellew's, and the other supporting the bundle on his shoulder, there appeared, galloping towards them, a man on a fine black horse, at sight of whom Porges' clasp tightened, and he drew nearer to Bellew's side.

When he was nearly abreast of them, the horse-man checked his career so suddenly that his animal was thrown back on his haunches.

"Why—George!" he exclaimed.

"Good-evening, Mr. Cassilis," said Small Porges, lifting his cap.

Mr. Cassilis was tall, handsome, well built, and very particular as to dress.

Bellew noticed that his teeth were indeed very large and white beneath the small, carefully trimmed moustache, and also his eyes seemed just a trifle too close together, perhaps.

"Why—what in the world have you been up to, boy?" he enquired, regarding Bellew with no friendly eye. "Your Aunt is worrying herself ill on your account! What have you been doing with yourself all day?"

Again Bellew felt the small fingers tighten round his, and the small figure shrink a little closer to him, as Small Porges answered:

"I've been with Uncle Porges, Mr. Cassilis."

"With whom?" demanded Mr. Cassilis sharply.

"With his Uncle Porges, Sir," Bellew rejoined. "A trustworthy person, and very much at your service."

"Uncle?" Mr. Cassilis repeated incredulously.

"Porges," said Bellew, nodding.

"I wasn't aware," began Mr. Cassilis, "that—er—George was so very fortunate . . ."

"Baptismal name—George," continued Bellew, "lately of New York, Newport, and—er—other places in America, U.S.A., at present of Nowhere-in-Particular."

"Ah," said Mr. Cassilis, his eyes seeming to grow a trifle nearer together, "an American Uncle? Still, I was not aware of even that relationship."

"It is a singularly pleasing thought," said Bellew, smiling, "to know that we may learn something every day. A very good afternoon to you, Sir. Come, nephew mine, the evening falls apace, and I grow weary. Let us on—Excelsior!"

Mr. Cassilis's cheek grew suddenly red. He twirled his moustache angrily, and seemed about to speak; then he smiled instead, and, turning his horse, spurred him savagely, and galloped back down the road in a cloud of dust.

Leaving the high-road, Small Porges guided Bellew by many winding paths through corn-fields and over stiles, until at length they came to an orchard.

In the midst of this orchard they stopped, and Small Porges rested one hand against the rugged bole of a great old apple tree.

"This," he said, "is my very own tree, because he's so very big, an' so very, very old. Adam says he's the oldest tree in the orchard. I call him King Arthur, 'cause he's so big an' strong—

just like a King should be, you know—an' all the other trees are his Knights of the Round Table."

But Bellew was not looking at "King Arthur," for just then his eyes were turned to where one came towards them through the green.

One surely as tall, gracious, proud, and beautiful as Enid, or Guinevere, or any of those lovely ladies, for all her simple gown of blue, and the sunbonnet that shaded the beauty of her face.

Yes, as he gazed, Bellew was sure and certain that she, who, all unconscious of their presence, came slowly towards them with the red glow of the sunset about her, was handsomer, lovelier, statelier, and altogether more desirable than all the beautiful ladies of King Arthur's Court.

But now Small Porges, finding him so silent, and seeing where he looked, gave a sudden, glad cry and ran out from behind the great bulk of "King Arthur."

On hearing his voice, she turned and ran to meet him, and sank upon her knees before him, and clasped him against her heart, and rejoiced, and wept, and scolded him, all in a breath.

Bellew, unobserved as yet in "King Arthur's" shadow, watched the proud head with its wayward curls (for the sunbonnet had been tossed back upon her shoulders), and watched the quick, passionate caress of those slender brown hands.

Listening to the thrilling tenderness of that low, soft voice, he felt all at once strangely lonely and friendless and out-of-place.

He also felt very rough and awkward, and very much aware of his dusty person—felt, indeed, as might any other ordinary human who had tumbled unexpectedly into Arcadia.

Therefore, he turned, thinking to steal quietly away.

"You see, Auntie, I went out to try an' find a fortune for you," Small Porges was explaining. "An' I looked an' looked, but I didn't find a bit ..."

"My dear, dear, brave Georgy!" Anthea smiled, and would have kissed him again, but he put her off.

"Wait a minute, please, Auntie," he said excitedly, "'cause I did find something. Just as I was growing very tired an' disappointed, I found Uncle Porges—under a hedge, you know."

"Uncle Porges?" Anthea asked. "Oh! That must be the man Mr. Cassilis mentioned ..."

"So I brought him with me," pursued Small Porges; "an' there he is."

He pointed triumphantly towards "King Arthur."

Glancing towards the tree, Anthea saw a tall, dusty figure moving off.

"Oh, wait ... please," she called, rising to her feet; and with Small Porges' hand in hers, she began to approach Bellew, who had stopped, with his dusty back to them.

"I ... want to thank you for ... taking care of my nephew. If you will come up to the house, Cook shall give you a good meal, and if you are in need of work, I ... I ..."

Her voice faltered uncertainly and she stopped.

"Thank you," said Bellew, turning and lifting his hat.

"Oh, I beg your pardon," said Anthea.

Now, as their eyes met, it seemed to Bellew

as though he had lived all his life in expectation
of this moment.

But now, even while he looked at her, he saw
her cheeks flush painfully and her dark eyes grow
troubled.

"I beg your pardon," she said again. "I . . . I
thought . . . Mr. Cassilis gave me to understand
that you were . . ."

"A very dusty, hungry-looking fellow, perhaps." Bellew smiled. "And he was quite right,
you know. The dust you can see for yourself, but
the hunger you must take my word for. As for the
work, I assure you exercise is precisely what I am
looking for."

"But . . ." Anthea said, and stopped, and
tapped the grass nervously with her foot, and
twisted one of her bonnet-strings, and, meeting
Bellew's steady gaze, flushed again.

"But you . . . you are . . ."

"My Uncle Porges," her nephew chimed in.
"An' I brought him home with me 'cause he's
going to help me to find a fortune; an' he hasn't
got any place to go to, 'cause his home's far, far
beyond the 'bounding billow.' So you will let
him stay, won't you, Auntie Anthea?"

"Why, Georgy," she began.

But, seeing her distressed look, Bellew came
to her rescue.

"Pray do, Miss Anthea," he said. "My name is
Bellew. I am an American, without family or
friends here, there, or anywhere; and with nothing
in the world to do but follow the path of the
winds.

"Indeed, I am rather a solitary fellow—at
least, I was, until I met my nephew Porges here.

Since then, I've been wondering if there would be—er—room for such as I at Dapplemere?"

"Oh, there would be plenty of room," Anthea said, hesitating, and wrinkling her white brow, for a lodger was something entirely new in her experience.

"As to my character," pursued Bellew, "though something of a vagabond, I am not a rogue—at least, I hope not, and I could pay—er—four or five pounds a week . . ."

"Oh!" exclaimed Anthea, with a little gasp.

"If that would be sufficient."

"It is . . . a great deal too much," Anthea replied, who would have scarcely dared to ask three.

"Pardon me, but I think not," said Bellew, shaking his head. "You see, I am—er—rather extravagant in my eating—eggs, you know, lots of them, and ham, and beef, and—er . . ."

(A duck quacked loudly from the vicinity of a neighbouring pond.)

"Certainly, an occasional duck. Indeed, five pounds a week would scarcely . . ."

"There would be ample," said Anthea, with a little nod of finality.

"Very well," said Bellew, "we'll make it four, and have done with it."

Four pounds a week! It would be a veritable Godsend just at present, while she was so hard put to it to make both ends meet.

Four pounds a week! So Anthea stood, lost in frowning thought, until, meeting his frank smile, she laughed.

"You are dreadfully persistent, and I know it is too much. But . . . we'll try to make you as comfortable as we can," she said, and she laid her hand in his.

Chapter
Two

Dapplemere Farm House, or The Manor, as it was still called by many, had been built when Henry the Eighth was King, as the carved inscription above the door testified.

As Bellew sat having his tea, he thought where in all this wide world could there ever be found just such another hostess as Miss Anthea herself?

"Milk and sugar, Mr. Bellew?"

"Thank you."

"This is blackberry, an' this is raspberry an' redcurrant . . . but the blackberry jam's the best, Uncle Porges."

"Thank you, nephew."

"Now, aren't you awful glad I found you under that hedge, Uncle Porges?"

"Nephew, I am."

"Nephew?" repeated Anthea, glancing at him with raised brows.

"Oh yes." Bellew nodded. "We adopted each other at about four o'clock this afternoon."

"Under a hedge, you know," added Small Porges.

"Wasn't it a very sudden and altogether un-heard-of proceeding?" Anthea enquired.

"Well, it might have been if it had happened anywhere but in Arcadia."

"What's Arcadia, Uncle Porges?"

"A place I've been looking for nearly all my life, nephew. I'll trouble you for the blackberry jam, my Porges."

"Yes, try the blackberry; Aunt Priscilla made it her very own self."

"You know, it's perfectly ridiculous," said An-thea, frowning and laughing, both at the same time.

"What is, Miss Anthea?"

"Why, that you should be sitting there call-ing Georgy your nephew, and that I should be pouring out tea for you, quite as a matter of course."

"And yet it seems to me to be the most de-lightfully natural thing in the world," Bellew said, and smiled in his slow, grave manner.

"But I've only known you half-an-hour!"

"But then, friendships ripen quickly in Ar-cadia."

"I wonder what Aunt Priscilla will have to say about it!"

"Aunt Priscilla?"

"She is our Housekeeper . . . the dearest, busi-est, gentlest little Housekeeper in all the world; but with very sharp eyes, Mr. Bellew. She will either like you very much, or not at all. There are no half-measures about Aunt Priscilla."

"Now, I wonder which it will be," said Bel-lew, helping himself to more jam.

"Oh, she'll like you, of course," said Small Porges, nodding. "I know she'll like you, 'cause you're so different from Mr. Cassilis. He's got black hair, an' a mestache, you know, an' your hair's gold, like mine, an' your mestache isn't there, is it? An' I know she doesn't like Mr. Cassilis, an' I don't either, 'cause . . ."

"She will be back tomorrow," said Anthea, silencing Porges with a gentle touch of her hand; "and we shall be glad, shan't we, Georgy? The house is not the same place without her."

She sighed before she went on:

"You see, I am off in the fields all day, as a rule; a farm, even such a small one as Dapplemere, is a great responsibility, and takes up all one's time, if it is to be made to pay."

"An' sometimes it doesn't pay at all, you know," added Small Porges. "An' then Auntie Anthea worries an' I worry too. Farming isn't what it was in Adam's young days—so that's why I must find a fortune—early tomorrow morning, you know, so my Auntie won't have to worry any more."

"It was very good and brave of you, dear," Anthea replied, and, leaning over, she kissed Small Porges suddenly, "to go out all alone into this big world to try and find a fortune for me."

She bent to kiss him again, but he reminded her that they were not alone.

"But, Georgy dear, fortunes are very hard to find, especially round Dapplemere, I'm afraid!"

"Yes; that's why I was going to Africa, you know."

"Africa!" she repeated. "Africa!"

"Oh yes." Bellew nodded. "When I met him he was on his way there to bring back gold for you in a sack."

"Only Uncle Porges said it was a goodish

way off, you know. So I 'cided to stay an' find the fortune nearer home."

They talked unaffectedly together until, tea being over, Anthea volunteered to show Bellew over her small domain, and they went out, all three, into an evening that breathed of roses and honeysuckle.

* * *

Bellew awakened early the next morning to find the sun pouring in through his window and making a glory all about him.

But it was not this that had awakened him, he thought, as he lay blinking drowsily, nor the blackbird piping so wonderfully in the apple tree outside. It was the sound of someone singing.

Bellew rose, crossed to the open casement, and leant out into the golden freshness of the morning.

Looking about, he presently saw the singer, who was none other than the Waggoner with whom he had fought and ridden on the preceding afternoon.

Bellew hailed him, and the man glanced up and, breaking off his song in the middle of a note, stood gazing at Bellew, open-mouthed.

"What, be that you, Sir?" he enquired at last. "Lord! An' what be you a-doing of up theer?"

"Why, sleeping, of course," answered Bellew.

"Wot, again!" exclaimed the Waggoner, with a grin. "You be forever a-sleepin', I do believe!"

"Not when you're anywhere about," said Bellew, laughing, as he went down and joined him.

"Was it me as woke ye, then?"

"Your singing did."

"My singin'! Lord love me, an' well it might! My singin' would wake the dead—leastways, so Prudence says, an' she's generally right! Leastways, if she ain't, she's a uncommon good cook, an' that goes a long way wi' most of us.

"But I don't sing very often, unless I be alone, or easy in my mind, an' 'appy-'earted—which I ain't."

"No?" enquired Bellew.

"No, by no manner o' means, I ain't. Contrariwise, my 'eart be sore an' full o' gloom—which ain't to be wondered at nohow."

"And yet you were singing."

"Ay, for sure, I were singin'. But then, who could help singin' on such a mornin' as this be."

Saying which, the Waggoner nodded suddenly and strode off.

Very soon Bellew was shaved and dressed, and, going downstairs, he let himself out into the early sunshine, and strolled away towards the farm-yard, where the Waggoner was feeding the animals.

"I think," said Bellew, as he came up, "I think you must be the Adam I have heard of."

"That be my name, Sir."

"Then, Adam, fill your pipe." Bellew extended his pouch, whereupon Adam thanked him, and, fishing a small, short, black clay pipe from his pocket, he proceeded to fill and light it.

"Yes, Sir," he nodded, inhaling the tobacco with much apparent enjoyment, "Adam I were baptized some thirty years ago, but I generally calls myself 'Old Adam.'"

"But you're not old, Adam."

"Why, it ain't on account o' my age, ye see, Sir; it be all because o' the 'Old Adam' as is in-

side o' me. Lord love ye! I am nat'rally that full o'
the 'Old Adam' as never was. An' 'e's always a
up an' taking of me at the shortest notice.

"Only t'other day he up an' took me because
Job Jagway ('e works for Squire Cassilis, you'll
understand, Sir), because Job Jagway says as
our hay (meanin' Miss Anthea's hay, you'll understand, Sir) was mouldy; well, the 'Old Adam' up
an' took me to that extent, Sir, that they 'ad to
carry Job Jagway home arterwards."

"And what did the Squire have to say about
your spoiling his man?"

"Wrote to Miss Anthea, o' course, Sir—he's
always writing to Miss Anthea about summat or
other. Says as how he was minded to lock me up
for 'sault an' battery, but, out o' respect for her, 'e
would let me off wi' a warning."

"Miss Anthea worried, I suppose?"

"Worried, Sir! 'Oh, Adam,' says she, 'oh,
Adam! 'Aven't I got enough to bear but you must
make it 'arder for me?' An' I see the tears in her
eyes while she said it.

"Me, make it 'arder for her! Jest as if I
wouldn't make things lighter for 'er if I could—
which I can't. Jest as if, to help Miss Anthea, I
wouldn't let 'em take me an'—well, never mind
what—only I would."

"Yes, I'm sure you would." Bellew nodded.
"And is the Squire over here at Dapplemere very
often, Adam?"

"Why, not so much lately, Sir. Last time were
yesterday, jest afore Master Georgy came 'ome.
I were at work here in the yard, an' Squire comes
riding up to me, smiling quite friendly like—
which were pretty good of him, considering as
Job Jagway ain't back to work yet.

" 'Oh, Adam,' says he, 'so you're 'aving a sale here at Dapplemere, are you?' Meaning, Sir, a sale of some bits an' sticks o' furniture as Miss Anthea's forced to part wi' to meet some bill or other.

" 'Summat o' that, Sir,' says I, making as light of it as I could. 'Why then, Adam,' says he, 'if Job Jagway should 'appen to come over to buy a few o' the things—no more fighting,' says 'e. An' so he nods an' smiles, an' off he rides.

"An', Sir, as I watched him go, the 'Old Adam' riz up in me to that extent as it's mercy I didn't have no pitchfork 'andy."

"So that was why you were feeling gloomy, was it, Adam?"

"Ah, an' enough to make any man feel gloomy, I should think. Miss Anthea's brave enough, but I reckon 'twill come nigh breakin' 'er 'eart to see the old stuff sold—the furniture an' that. So she's goin' to drive over to Crankbrook, to be out o' the way while it's a-doin'.' "

"And when does the sale take place?"

"The Saturday after next, Sir, as ever was," Adam answered. "But, hush! Mum's the word, Sir!"

He broke off, and, winking violently, with a sideways motion of the head, he took up his pitchfork.

Glancing round, Bellew saw Anthea coming towards them, fresh and sweet as the morning.

"Good-morning," Bellew said. "You are early abroad this morning."

"Early, Mr. Bellew? Why, I've been up for hours. I'm generally out at four o'clock on market-days. We work hard and long at Dapplemere," she answered, giving him her hand with her grave, sweet smile.

"Aye, for sure," said Adam, nodding. "But farmin' ain't what it was in my young days."

"But I think we shall do well with the hops, Adam."

"'Ops, Miss Anthea! Lord love me! There ain't no 'ops nowhere as good as ourn be!"

"They ought to be ready for picking soon. Do you think thirty people will be enough?"

"Ah! They'll be more'n enough, Miss Anthea."

"And, Adam, the five-acre field should be mowed today."

"I'll set the men at it right arter breakfast; I'll 'ave it done, trust me, Miss Anthea."

"I do, Adam . . . you know that."

And with a smiling nod she turned away.

As Bellew walked on beside her, he felt a strange constraint upon him, such as he had never experienced towards any woman before.

"Do you like Dapplemere, Mr. Bellew?"

"Like it?" he repeated. "Like it? Yes indeed."

"I'm so glad," she answered, her eyes glowing with pleasure.

"You must be very fond of such a beautiful place."

"Oh, I love it!" she cried passionately. "If ever I had to give it up, I think I should die!"

She stopped suddenly, and, as though somewhat abashed by this outburst, added in a lighter tone:

"If I seem rather tragic it is because this is the only home I have ever known."

"Well," replied Bellew, appearing rather more dreamy than usual just then, "I have journeyed here and there in this world of ours, I have wandered up and down and to and fro in it, yet I never saw or dreamt of any such place as this Dapplemere of yours.

"It is Arcadia itself, and only I am out-of-place. I seem, somehow, to be too common-place, and altogether matter-of-fact."

"I'm sure I'm matter-of-fact enough," she answered with her low, sweet laugh, which Bellew thought was all too rare.

"You?" he said, and shook his head.

"Well?" she enquired, glancing at him through her wind-tossed curls.

"You are like some fair and stately lady out of the old romances."

"In a print gown and sunbonnet?"

"Even so." He nodded.

Here, for no apparent reason, the colour deepened in her cheeks, and she was silent.

"You, surely, are the Princess ruling this fair land of Arcadia, and I am the Stranger within your gates. It behoves you, therefore, to be merciful to this Stranger, if only for the sake of—er—our mutual nephew."

Whatever Anthea might have said in answer was cut short by Small Porges himself, who came galloping towards them, with the sun bright in his curls.

"Oh, Uncle Porges," he said, panting, as he came up. "I was afraid you'd gone away an' left me. I've been hunting an' hunting for you ever since I got up."

"No, I haven't gone away yet, my Porges."

"An' you won't go, ever or ever, will you?"

"That," said Bellew, taking the small hand in his, "that is a question that we had better leave to the—er—future, nephew."

"But why?"

"Well, you see, it doesn't rest with me, altogether, my Porges."

"Then who . . ." he was beginning; but Anthea's soft voice interrupted him.

"Georgy dear, didn't Prudence send you to tell us that breakfast was ready?"

"Oh, yes. I was forgetting—awful silly of me, wasn't it? But you are going to stay—oh, a long, long time, aren't you, Uncle Porges?"

"I sincerely hope so," answered Bellew.

Now, as he spoke, his eyes—by the merest chance in the world, of course—happened to meet Anthea's, whereupon she turned, and slipped on her sunbonnet, which she held in her hand.

This was very natural, for the sun was growing hot already.

"I'm awful glad," said Small Porges, sighing, "an' Auntie's glad, too, aren't you, Auntie?"

"Why, of course," came the reply, from the depths of the sunbonnet.

"'Cause now, you see, there'll be two of us to take care of you; Uncle Porges is so nice an' big, an' wide, isn't he, Auntie?"

"Y-e-s. Oh, Georgy! What are you talking about?"

"Why, I mean I'm rather small to take care of you all by myself alone, Auntie, though I do my best, of course. But now that I've found myself a big, tall Uncle Porges—under the hedge, you know—we can take care of you together, can't we, Auntie Anthea?"

But Anthea only hurried on without speaking, whereupon Small Porges continued:

"You 'member the other night, Auntie, when you were crying, you said you wished you had someone very big and strong to take care of you . . ."

"Oh, Georgy!"

Bellew heartily wished that sunbonnets had never been thought of.

"But you did, you know, Auntie. An' so that was why I went out an' found Uncle Porges for you—so that he . . ."

But here Mistress Anthea, for all her pride and stateliness, catching her gown about her, fairly ran on down the path, and never paused until she had reached the cool, dim parlour.

Being there, she tossed aside her sunbonnet, and looked at herself in the long, old mirror. And, though surely no mirror made by man ever reflected a fairer vision of dark-eyed witchery and loveliness, nevertheless Anthea stamped her foot and frowned at it.

"Oh, Georgy!" she exclaimed, and covered her burning cheeks.

Meanwhile, Big Porges and Small Porges, walking along hand in hand, shook their heads solemnly, wondering much upon the capriciousness of Aunts, and the waywardness thereof.

"I wonder why she runned away, Uncle Porges."

"Ah, I wonder."

"Specks she's a bit angry with me, you know, 'cause I told you she was crying."

"Hm," said Bellew.

"An Auntie takes an awful lot of looking-after," said Small Porges, with a sigh.

"Yes." Bellew nodded. "I suppose so—especially if she happens to be young and—er . . ."

"An' what, Uncle Porges?"

"Beautiful, nephew?"

"Oh! Do you think she is really beautiful?" demanded Small Porges.

"I'm afraid I do," Bellew confessed.

"So does Mr. Cassilis. I heard him tell her so once—in the orchard."

"Hm," said Bellew.

"Ah! But you ought to see her when she comes to tuck me up at night, with her hair all down an' hanging all about her, like a shiny cloak, you know."

"Hm!" Bellew said again.

"Please, Uncle Porges," said Georgy, turning to look up at him, "what makes you 'hm' so much this morning?"

"I was thinking, my Porges."

" 'Bout my Auntie Anthea?"

"I do admit the soft impeachment, Sir."

"Well, I'm thinking, too."

"What is it, old chap?"

"I'm thinking we ought to begin to find that fortune for her after breakfast."

"Why, it isn't quite the right season for fortune-hunting, yet—at least, not in Arcadia," answered Bellew, shaking his head.

"Oh, but why not?"

"Well, the moon isn't right, for one thing."

"The moon!" echoed Small Porges.

"Oh yes; we must wait for a—er—a Money Moon, you know. Surely you've heard of a Money Moon?"

" 'Fraid not." Small Porges sighed regretfully. "But I've heard of a Honey Moon . . ."

"They're often much the same," said Bellew, nodding.

"But when will the Money Moon come, an' how?"

"I can't exactly say, my Porges; but come it will, one of these fine nights. And when it does, we shall know that the fortune is close-by, and waiting to be found. So don't worry your small head about it. Just keep your eye on your Uncle."

*   *   *

Small Porges was at his lessons, and Bellew, watching, where he stood outside the window, noticed that Anthea frowned as she bent over her accounts and sighed wearily more than once.

It was after a sigh, rather more hopeless than usual, that, chancing to raise her eyes, they encountered those of the watcher outside, who, seeing himself discovered, smiled and came to lean in at the open window.

"Won't they balance?" he enquired, with a nod towards the heap of bills and papers before her.

"Oh yes," she answered, with a rueful little smile, "but ... on the wrong side, if you know what I mean."

"I know." He nodded, watching how her lashes curled against her cheek.

"If only we had done better with our first crop of hay," she said with a sigh.

"Job Jagway said it was mouldy, you know, that's why Adam punched him in the ..."

"Georgy ... go on with your work, Sir."

"Yes, Auntie."

"I'm building all my hopes this year on the hops," said Anthea, sinking her head upon her hand; "if they should fail ..."

"Well?" enquired Bellew, with his gaze upon the soft curve of her throat.

"I daren't think of it."

"Then don't. Let us talk of something else!"

"Yes, of Aunt Priscilla," Anthea nodded; "she is in the garden."

"And pray, who is Aunt Priscilla?"

"Go and meet her."

"But . . ."

"Go and find her . . . in the orchard," repeated Anthea. "Oh, do go, and leave us to our work."

So, turning obediently into the orchard, and looking about, Bellew presently saw a little, bright-eyed old lady who sat beneath the shadow of "King Arthur," with a rustic table beside her, upon which stood a basket of sewing.

Now, as he went, he chanced to spy a ball of worsted that had fallen, and, stooping, he picked it up, while she watched him with her quick, bright eyes.

"Good-morning, Mr. Bellew," she said, in response to his salutation. "It was nice of you to trouble to pick up an old woman's ball of worsted."

As she spoke, she rose and dropped him a curtsey; and then, as he looked at her again, he saw that despite her words, and despite her white hair, she was much younger and prettier than he had thought.

"I am Miss Anthea's Housekeeper," she went on. "I was away when you arrived, looking after one of Miss Anthea's old ladies. Pray, be seated.

"Miss Anthea, bless her dear heart, calls me her Aunt, but I'm not really, oh, dear no! I'm no relation at all."

She smiled at him and continued:

"But I've lived with her long enough to feel as if I were her Aunt, and her Uncle, and her Father, and her Mother, all rolled into one, though I should be rather small to be so many, shouldn't I?"

She laughed so gaily and unaffectedly that Bellew laughed too.

"I tell you all this," she went on, keeping pace to her flying needle, "because I have taken a fancy to you, on the spot. I always like or dislike a person on the spot—first impressions, you know!

"Y-e-s," she continued, glancing up at him sideways, "I like you just as much as I dislike Mr. Cassilis! How I do detest that man! There, now that's off my mind."

"And why?" enquired Bellew, smiling.

"Dear me, Mr. Bellew, how should I know, only I do; and what's more, he knows it too! And how," she enquired, changing the subject abruptly, "how is your bed, comfortable?"

"Very."

"You sleep well?"

"Like a top."

"Any complaints so far?"

"None whatever," replied Bellew, laughing as he shook his head.

"That is very well. We have never had a boarder before, and Miss Anthea, bless her dear soul, was a little nervous about it. And here's the Sergeant."

"I—er—beg your pardon?" said Bellew.

"The Sergeant," repeated Miss Priscilla, with a prim little nod, "Sergeant Appleby, late of the Nineteenth Hussars, a soldier every inch of him, Mr. Bellew, with one arm, over there by the peaches."

Glancing in the direction she indicated, Bellew observed a tall figure.

"The very first thing he will say will be, 'It is a very fine day,' " said Miss Priscilla with a nod, stitching away faster than ever; "and the next, 'The peaches are doing very well,' now mark my words, Mr. Bellew."

As she spoke, the Sergeant came striding towards them, juggling imaginary spurs, and with his stick tucked up under his remaining arm, very much as if it were a sabre.

"A particularly fine day, Miss Priscilla, for the time o' the year," he said.

"Indeed, I quite agree with you, Sergeant," returned little Miss Priscilla, with a bright nod, and a sly glance at Bellew, as much as to say, "I told you so."

"And the peaches, Mam," continued the Sergeant, "the peaches never looked better, Mam."

Having said which, he stood looking at nothing in particular, with his one hand resting lightly on his hip.

"Yes, to be sure, Sergeant," said Miss Priscilla, with another sly look. "But let me introduce you to Mr. Bellew, who is staying at Dapplemere."

"Proud to know you, Sir—your servant, Sir!"

"How do you do?" Bellew replied with his frank smile, and held out his hand.

The Sergeant hesitated, then put out his remaining hand.

"My left, Sir," he said apologetically. "Can't be helped; left my right out in India, a good many years ago. Good place for soldiering, India, Sir—plenty of active service—chances of promotion—though the sun is bad!"

"Sergeant," said Miss Priscilla, "sit down, do."

"Thank you, Mam," he smiled, and proceeded to seat himself at the other end of the rustic bench. "And how might Miss Anthea be?"

"Oh, very well, thank you," said Miss Priscilla, nodding.

"Good!" exclaimed the Sergeant. "Very good!

"And how," he went on after a moment, "how might Master Georgy be?"

"Master Georgy is as well as ever," answered Miss Priscilla, stitching away faster than before, and Bellew thought she kept her rosy cheeks stooped a little lower over her work.

"And pray, Mam," said the Sergeant, "how might you be feeling, Mam?"

"Much the same as usual, thank you," she answered, smiling like a girl, for all her white hair, as the Sergeant's eyes met hers.

"You look," he said, pausing to cough behind his hand, "you look blooming, Mam—if you'll allow the expression—blooming—as you ever do, Mam."

"I'm an old woman, Sergeant, as well you know!" said Miss Priscilla with a sigh, shaking her head.

"Old, Mam!" repeated the Sergeant. "Old, Mam! Nothing of the sort, Mam! Age has nothing to do with it. 'Tisn't the years as count. We aren't any older than we feel—eh, Sir?"

"Of course not," answered Bellew.

"Nor than we look—eh, Sir?"

"Certainly not, Sergeant," answered Bellew.

"And she, Sir, she doesn't look a day older than . . ."

"Thirty-five," said Bellew.

"Exactly, Sir, very true! My own opinion, thirty-five exactly, Sir."

He coughed.

"Must be going," he said after a moment, standing very straight and looking down at little Miss Priscilla, "though sorry as ever—must be going, Mam—Miss Priscilla, Mam—good day to you."

And he stretched out his hand to her with a sudden, jerky movement.

Miss Priscilla paused in her sewing and looked up at him with her youthful smile.

"Must you go so soon, Sergeant? Then good-bye until tomorrow," she said, and laid her very small hand in his big palm.

The Sergeant stared down at it as though he were greatly minded to raise it to his lips, but instead he dropped it suddenly and turned to Bellew.

"Sir, I am proud to have met you. Sir, there is a poor crippled soldier as I know—his cottage is very small, and humble, Sir, but if you ever feel like dropping in on him, Sir, by day or night, he will be honoured, Sir, honoured!"

He coughed.

"And that's me, Sergeant Richard Appleby— late of the Nineteenth Hussars, at your service, Sir!" Saying which, he put on his hat, stiff-armed, wheeled, and strode away through the orchard.

"Well?" enquired Miss Priscilla, in her quick, bright way. "Well, Mr. Bellew, what do you think of him—first impressions are always best—at least, I think so—what do you think of Sergeant Appleby?"

"I think he's a splendid fellow," said Bellew, looking after the Sergeant's upright figure.

"A very foolish old fellow, I think, and as stiff as one of the ram-rods of one of his own guns," said Miss Priscilla, but her clear blue eyes were very soft and tender as she spoke.

"And as fine a soldier as a man, I'm sure," said Bellew.

"Why, yes, he was a good soldier, once upon a time, I believe; he won the Victoria Cross for doing something or other that was very brave, and he wears it with all his other medals, pinned on the inside of his coat.

"Oh yes, he was a fine soldier, once; but he's a very foolish old soldier now, I think. But I'm glad you like him, Mr. Bellew, and he will be proud and happy for you to call and see him at his cottage. And now, I suppose, it is half-past eleven, isn't it?"

"Yes, just half-past." Bellew nodded, glancing at his watch.

"Exact to time, as usual," said Miss Priscilla. "I don't think the Sergeant has missed a minute, or varied a minute, in the last five years; you see, he is such a very methodical man, Mr. Bellew!"

"Why, then, does he come every day at the same hour?"

"Every day," replied Miss Priscilla, nodding. "It has become a matter of habit with him."

"Ah?" said Bellew, smiling.

"If you were to ask me why he comes, I should answer that I fancy it is to look at the peaches. Dear me, Mr. Bellew, what a very foolish old soldier he is, to be sure!"

Saying which, pretty, bright-eyed Miss Priscilla laughed again, folded up her work, settled it in the basket with a deft little pat, and, rising, took a small crutch-stick from where it had lain concealed, and then Bellew saw that she was lame.

"Oh yes, I'm a cripple, you see." She nodded. "Oh, very, very lame—my ankle, you know. That is why I came here. The big world didn't want a poor lame old woman, and that is why Miss Anthea made me her Aunt. God bless her!

"No, thank you, I can carry my basket. So you see, he has lost an arm, his right one, and I am lame in my foot. Perhaps that is why... Heigho! How beautifully the blackbirds are singing this morning, to be sure!"

*   *   *

Anthea, leaning on her rake in a shady corner of the field, turned to watch Bellew, who, stripped to his shirt-sleeves, bare of neck and arm, and pitchfork in hand, was busy tossing up mounds of sweet-smelling hay to Adam, who stood upon a great waggon to receive it, with Small Porges perched up beside him.

A week had elapsed since Bellew had found his way to Dapplemere, a week which had only served to strengthen the bonds of affection between him and his "nephew," and to win over sharp-eyed, shrewd little Miss Priscilla to the extent of declaring him to be:

"First a gentleman, Anthea, my dear; and secondly, what is much rarer nowadays, a true man!"

A week, and already he was a hail-fellow-well-met with everyone about the place, for who was proof against his unaffected gaiety, and his simple, easy, good fellowship?

So he laughed and joked as he swung his pitchfork (awkwardly enough, to be sure) and received all hints and directions as to its use, in the kindly spirit they were tendered.

And Anthea, watching him from her shady corner, sighed once or twice, and, catching herself so doing, stamped her foot at herself and pulled her sunbonnet closer about her face.

"No, Adam," he was saying, "depend upon it, there is nothing like exercise, and, of all exercise, give me a pitchfork."

Then, turning his head, Bellew espied Anthea watching him, whereupon he shouldered his fork, and, coming to where she sat upon a throne of hay, he sank down at her feet with a luxurious sigh.

She had never seen him without a collar before, and now she could not but notice how round and white and powerful his neck was, and how the muscles bulged upon arm and shoulder, and how his hair curled in small damp rings upon his brow.

"It is good," he said, looking up into the bewitching face above him, "yes, it is very good to see you idle—just for once."

"And I was thinking it was good to see you work . . . just for once."

"Work!" he exclaimed. "My dear Miss Anthea, I assure you, I am becoming a positive glutton for work. It has become my earnest desire to plant things, and grow things, and chop things with axes, and mow things with scythes.

"By night I dream of pastures and ploughs, of pails and pitchforks, and by day, reaping-hooks,

hoes, and rakes are in my thoughts continually—
which all goes to show the effect of this wonderful air of Arcadia."

"How ridiculous you are!" she said, laughing.

"And how perfectly content!" he added.

"Is anyone ever quite content?" She sighed,
glancing down at him wistful-eyed.

"Not unless they have found Arcadia," he
answered.

"Have you then?"

"Yes," he nodded complacently, "oh yes, I've
found it."

"Are you . . . sure?"

"Quite sure."

"Arcadia!" she repeated, wrinkling her brows.
"What is Arcadia, and . . . where?"

"Arcadia," answered Bellew, watching the
smoke rise up from his pipe, with a dreamy eye,
"Arcadia is the Promised Land—the Land that
everyone tries to find, sometime or other, and
may be—anywhere."

"And how did you find it?"

"By the most fortunate chance in the world."

"Tell me," said Anthea, taking a wisp of hay
and beginning to plait it with her dexterous brown
fingers, "tell me how you found it."

"Why then, in the first place, you must
know," he began, in his slow, even voice, "that it
is a place I have sought for in all my wanderings
—and I have been pretty far afield; but I sought
it so long and so vainly that I began to think it
was like the El Dorado of the old adventures, and
had never existed at all."

"Yes?" said Anthea, busy with her plaiting.

"But one day, Fate or Chance, or Destiny—

or their benevolent spirit—sent a certain square-shouldered Waggoner to show me the way, and after him, a very small Porges—bless him—to lead me into this wonderful Arcadia."

"Oh, I see!" Anthea nodded, very intent upon her plaiting.

"But there is something more," said Bellew.

"Oh?" enquired Anthea.

"Shall I tell you?"

"If . . . it is . . . very interesting."

"Well then, in this delightful land there is a castle, grim, embattled, and very strong."

"A castle?" said Anthea, glancing up suddenly.

"The Castle of Heart's Desire."

"Oh!" she said, and gave all her attention to her plaiting again.

"And so," continued Bellew, "I am waiting very patiently until, in her own good time, she who rules within shall open the gate to me, or bid me go away."

Into Bellew's voice had crept a thrill no-one had ever heard there before; he leant nearer to her, and his dreamy eyes were keen and eager now.

And she, though she saw nothing of all this, yet being a woman, knew it was there, of course, and for that very reason looked resolutely away.

Once again Bellew wished that sunbonnets had never been invented!

So there was silence while Anthea stared across the golden corn-fields, yet saw nothing of them, and Bellew looked upon those slender, capable fingers that had faltered in their plaiting and stopped. And thus upon the silence there broke a sudden voice, shrill with interest.

"Go on. Uncle Porges, what about the dragons? Oh, please go on—why, there's always dragons in 'chanted castles, you know, to guard the lovely Princess. Oh, do please have a dragon."

And Small Porges appeared from the other side of the hay-mow, flushed and eager.

"Certainly, my Porges." Bellew nodded, drawing the small figure down beside him. "I was forgetting the dragons, but there they are, with scaly backs, and iron claws, spitting out sparks and flames, just as self-respecting dragons should, and roaring away like thunder."

"Ah!" exclaimed Small Porges, nestling closer to Bellew and reaching out a hand to Auntie Anthea, "that's fine, let's have plenty of dragons."

"Do you think a—er—dozen would be enough, my Porges?"

"Oh, yes! But s'pose the beautiful Princess didn't open the door—what would you do if you were really a wandering Knight who was waiting patiently for it to open—what would you do then?"

"Shin up a tree, my Porges."

"Oh, but that wouldn't be a bit right, would it, Auntie?"

"Of course not," said Anthea, laughing, "it would be most unknightlike, and very undignified."

"'Sides," added Small Porges, "you couldn't climb up a tree in your armour, you know."

"Then I'd make an awful good try at it!" said Bellew.

"No," said Small Porges, shaking his head. "Shall I tell you what you ought to do? Well then, you'd draw your two-edged sword, an' dress your shield—like Gareth, the Kitchen Knave, did, he was always dressing his shield, an' so was Lancelot—an' you'd fight all those dragons an' kill them an' cut their heads off."

"And then what would happen?" enquired Bellew.

"Why, then the lovely Princess would open the gate, an' marry you, of course, an' live happy ever after, an' all would be revelry an' joy."

"Ah!" Bellew sighed. "If she'd do that, I think I'd fight all the dragons that ever roared, and kill them too. But supposing she—er—wouldn't open the gate?"

"Why, then," said Small Porges, wrinkling his brow, "why, then—you'd have to storm the castle, of course, an' break open the gate an' run off with the Princess on your charger—if she was very beautiful, you know."

"A most excellent idea, my Porges! If I should happen to find myself in like circumstances, I'll surely take your advice."

Now, as he spoke, Bellew glanced at Anthea, and she at him. And straightaway she blushed, and then she laughed, and then she blushed again, and, still blushing, rose to her feet and turned to find Mr. Cassilis within a yard of them.

"Ah, Miss Anthea," he said, lifting his hat. "I sent Georgy to find you, but it seems that he forgot to mention that I was waiting."

"I'm awful' sorry, Mr. Cassilis, but Uncle Porges was telling us 'bout dragons, you know," Small Porges hastened to explain.

"Dragons!" repeated Mr. Cassilis, with his supercilious smile. "Ah, indeed! Dragons should be interesting, especially in such a very quiet, shady nook as this—quite an idyllic place for story-telling; it's a positive shame to disturb you."

His sharp white teeth gleamed beneath his moustache as he spoke, and he tapped his riding-boot lightly with his hunting-crop as he fronted Bellew, who had risen, and stood bare-armed, leaning upon his pitchfork.

And, as in their first meeting, there was a mute antagonism in their look.

"Let me introduce you to each other," said Anthea, conscious of this attitude. "Mr. Cassilis, of Brampton Court . . . Mr. Bellew."

"Of nowhere in particular, Sir," added Bellew.

"And pray," said Mr. Cassilis perfunctorily, as they strolled on across the meadow, "how do you like Dapplemere, Mr. Bellew?"

"Immensely, Sir—beyond all expression!"

"Yes, it is considered rather pretty, I believe."

"Lovely, Sir!" replied Bellew. "Though it is not so much the beauty of the place itself that appeals to me as what it contains."

"Oh, indeed!" said Mr. Cassilis, with a sudden sharp glance. "To what do you refer?"

"Gooseberries, Sir."

"I—ah—beg your pardon."

"Sir," said Bellew, gravely; "all my life I have fostered a secret passion for gooseberries—raw or cooked—in pie, pudding, or jam, they are equally alluring. Unhappily, the American gooseberry is but a hollow mockery, at best . . ."

"Ha," replied Mr. Cassilis, dubiously.

"Now, in gooseberries, as in everything else, Sir, there is to be found the superlative, the quintessence—the ideal. Consequently, I have roamed east and west, and north and south, in quest of it."

"Really?" responded Mr. Cassilis, stifling a

yawn, and turned towards Miss Anthea, with the very slightest shrug of his shoulders.

"And in Dapplemere," concluded Bellew, solemnly, "I have at last found my ideal . . ."

"Gooseberry," added Anthea, with a laugh in her eyes.

"Arcadia being a land of ideals," said Bellew, nodding.

"Ideals," said Mr. Cassilis, caressing his moustache, "ideals and—ah—gooseberries, though probably excellent things in themselves, are apt to pall upon one, in time; personally, I find them equally insipid."

"Of course it is all a matter of taste," said Bellew, sighing.

"But," Cassilis went on, fairly turning his back upon him, "the subject I wished to discuss with you, Miss Anthea, was the—er—approaching sale."

"The sale!" she repeated, all the brightness dying out of her face.

"I wished," said Cassilis, leaning nearer to her, and lowering his voice confidentially, "to try to convince you how unnecessary it would be—if . . ."

He paused, significantly.

Anthea turned quickly aside, as though to hide her mortification from Bellew's keen eyes; whereupon he, seeing it all, became straightaway more dreamy than ever.

He laid a hand upon Small Porges' shoulder, and pointed with his pitchfork to where at the other end of the "five-acre" the haymakers were working away as merrily as ever.

"Come, my Porges, let us away and join the happy throng, and—er . . .

" 'With Daphnis, and Clo, and Blowsabel,
We'll listen to the—er—cuckoo in the dell.' "

So, hand in hand, the two Porges set off
together.

But, when they had gone some distance, Bellew looked back and saw that although Anthea
walked with her head averted, Cassilis was close
beside her, and stooped, now and then, until the
black moustache came very near the curl—that
curl of wanton witchery that peeped above her
ear.

"Uncle Porges—why do you frown so?"

"Frown, my Porges, did I? Well, I was thinking."

"Well, I'm thinking too, only I don't frown,
you know, but I'm thinking just the same."

"And what might you be thinking, nephew?"

"Why, I was thinking that although you're
so awful fond of gooseberries, an' though there's
still some ripe ones on the bushes, I've never
seen you eat a single one."

Chapter
Three

"Look at the moon tonight, Uncle Porges!"

"I see it."

"It's awful' big an' round, isn't it?"

"Yes, it's very big and very round."

"An' rather yellow, isn't it?"

"Very yellow."

"Just like a great big golden sovereign, isn't it?"

"Very much like a sovereign, my Porges."

"Well, do you know, I was wondering if there was any chance that it was a Money Moon."

They were leaning out at the lattice, Small Porges and Big Porges.

Anthea and Miss Priscilla were busy upon household matters wholly feminine, wherefore Small Porges had drawn Bellew to the window, and there they leant, the small body enfolded by Bellew's long arm, and the two faces turned up to the silvery splendour of the moon.

But now Anthea came up behind them, and, not noticing the position of Bellew's arm as she leant on the other side of Small Porges, it happened that her hand touched and for a moment rested upon Bellew's hand, hidden as it was in the shadow.

"And pray," said Anthea, laying that same hand in the most natural manner in the world upon Small Porges' curls, "pray, what might you two be discussing so very solemnly?"

"The moon," answered Small Porges. "I was wondering if it was a Money Moon, an' Uncle Porges hasn't said if it is yet."

"Why no, old chap," answered Bellew. "I'm afraid not."

"And pray," said Anthea again, "what might a Money Moon be?"

"Well," explained Small Porges, "when the moon's just—just so, then you go out an'—an' find a fortune, you know. But the moon's got to be a Money Moon, and you've got to know, you know, else you'll find nothing, of course."

"Ah, George dear!" Anthea sighed, stooping her dark head down to his coppery curls. "Don't you know that fortunes are very hard to get, and that they have to be worked for, and that no-one ever found one without a great deal of labour and sorrow?"

"Course, everyone can't find fortunes, Auntie Anthea, I know that, but we shall; my Uncle Porges knows all about it, you see, an' I know that we shall. I'm sure as sure we shall find one, someday, 'cause you see, I put it in my prayers now—at the end, you know. I say:

" 'An' please help me an' my Uncle Porges to find a fortune, when the Money Moon comes— a big one—world without end—Amen.' So you see, it's all right, an' we're just waiting till the Money Moon comes, aren't we, Uncle Porges?"

"Yes, old chap, yes," Bellew nodded, "until the Money Moon comes."

There fell a silence between them, yet a silence that held a wondrous charm of its own; a silence that lasted so long that the coppery curls drooped lower and lower upon Bellew's arm, until Anthea, sighing, rose, and in a very tender voice bade Small Porges say "good-night."

This he did, and, sleepy-eyed, with his hand in Anthea's, went drowsily up to bed.

Bellew sauntered out into the rose-garden to look upon the beauty of the night.

He came across Adam, who started talking about the sale.

"Ah yes, the sale," said Bellew, thoughtfully.

"To think o' that there Job Jagway a-coming over here to buy Miss Anthea's furniture do set the Old Adam a-workin' inside o' me to that amazin' extent as I can't sit still, Mr. Belloo, Sir! If that there Job crosses my path tomorrow—well —let 'im look out, that's all!"

"Adam," said Bellew, in the same thoughtful tone, "I wonder, would you do something for me?"

"Anything you ax me, Sir, so long as you don't want me to . . ."

"I want you to buy some of that furniture for me."

"What!" exclaimed Adam, and vented his great laugh again. "Well, if that ain't a good 'un, Sir! Why, that's just what I'm a-going to do.

"You see, I ain't wot you might call a rich man, nor yet a millionaire, but I've got a bit put by, an' I drawed out ten pounds yesterday."

He stroked his head before he continued:

"Thinks I—here's to save Miss Anthea's old sideboard, or the mirror she's so fond of, or if not—why then, a chair or so—they ain't a-going to get it all—not while I've got a pound or two, I says to myself."

"Adam," said Bellew, turning suddenly, "that sentiment does you credit. But now I want you to put back your ten pounds, keep it for Prudence, whom I know you want to wed, because I happen to have rather more than we shall want. See here!"

With the words, Bellew took out a bundle of bank-notes from a leather wallet. There was more money than Adam had ever seen in all his thirty-odd years. Seeing it, his eyes opened wide, and his square jaw relaxed, to the imminent danger of his cherished clay pipe.

"I want you to take this," Bellew went on, counting a sum into Adam's nerveless hand, "and tomorrow, when the sale begins, if anyone makes a bid for anything, I want you to bid higher, and no matter what, you must always buy—always, you understand?"

"But, Sir, that there old drorin'-room cab'net wi' the carvings . . ."

"Buy it."

"An' the silver candle-sticks, and the four-post bedstead, an' the . . ."

"Buy them, Adam, buy everything! If we haven't enough money, there's plenty more where this came from—only buy. You understand?"

"Oh yes, Sir, I understand! 'Ow much 'ave you give me? Why, here's forty-five—fifty—sixty —Lord . . ."

"Put it away, Adam; forget all about it till tomorrow, and not a word, mind!"

"A hundred pounds!" said Adam, gasping. "Lord! Oh, I won't speak of it, trust me, Mr. Belloo, Sir! But to think of Old Adam—me—a-walking about wi' a hundred pound in my pocket, e' God! it does seem comical!"

Saying which, Adam buttoned the money into a capacious pocket, slapped it, nodded, and rose.

"Well, Sir, I'll be going—there be Miss Anthea in the garden yonder, and if she was to see me now, there's no sayin' but I should be took a laughin' to think o' this 'ere hundred pound."

"Miss Anthea—where?"

"Comin' through the rose-garden. She be off to see ole Mother Dibbin. They call Mother Dibbin a witch, an' now as she's down wi' the rheumatics there ain't nobody to look arter 'er— 'cept Miss Anthea."

Saying which, Adam slapped his pocket again, and went upon his way.

It is a moot question as to whether a curl is more alluring when it glows beneath the fiery kisses of the sun, or shines demurely in the tender radiance of the moon.

As Bellew looked at it now—that same curl that nodded and beckoned to him above Anthea's left ear—he strongly inclined to the latter opinion.

"Adam tells me that you are going out, Miss Anthea."

"Only as far as Mrs. Dibbin's cottage—just across the meadow."

"Adam also informs me that Mrs. Dibbin is a witch."

"People call her so."

"Never in all my days have I seen a genuine old witch, so I'll come with you, if I may?"

"Oh, this is a very gentle old witch, and she is neither hump-backed nor does she ride on a broomstick, so I'm afraid you'll be disappointed, Mr. Bellew."

"Then at least I can carry your basket—allow me."

In his quiet, masterful fashion he took the basket from her arm, and walked on beside her through the orchard.

"What a glorious night it is!" exclaimed Anthea, suddenly, drawing a deep breath of the fragrant air. "Oh, it is good to be alive! In spite of all the cares and worries, life is sweet!"

They walked on some distance in silence, she gazing wistfully upon the beauties of the familiar world about her, while he watched the curl above her ear until she, becoming aware of it all at once, promptly sent it back into retirement with a quick, deft little pat of her fingers.

"I hope," said Bellew at last, "I do sincerely hope that you 'tucked-up' my nephew safely in bed. You see . . ."

"Your nephew, indeed!"

"Our nephew, then. I ask because he tells me that he can't possibly sleep unless you go to 'tuck him up'—and I can quite believe it."

"Do you know, Mr. Bellew, I'm growing quite jealous of you; he can't move a step without you, and he is forever talking of you and lauding your numberless virtues."

"But then, I'm only an Uncle, after all; and if he talks of me to you, he talks of you to me all day long."

"Oh, does he?"

"And among other things, he told me that I

ought to see you when your hair is down and all about you."

"Oh!" exclaimed Anthea.

"Indeed, our nephew is much luckier than I, because I never had an Aunt of my own to come and 'tuck me up' at night with her hair hanging all about her—like a beautiful cloak. So, you see, I have no boyish recollections to go upon, but I think I can imagine . . ."

"And what do you think of the Sergeant?" Anthea enquired, changing the subject abruptly.

"I like him so much that I am going to take him at his word and call upon him at the first opportunity."

"Did Aunt Priscilla tell you that he comes marching along regularly every day, at exactly the same hour?"

"Yes, to see how the peaches are getting on!" Bellew nodded.

"For such a very brave soldier, he is a dreadful coward," Anthea said with a smile. "It has taken him five years to screw up courage enough to tell her that she's uncommonly young for her age. And yet I think it is just that very diffidence that makes him so lovable.

"He is so simple and so gentle—in spite of all his war medals. When I am moody and cross, the very sight of him is enough to put me in humour again."

"Has he never spoken to Miss Priscilla?"

"Never; though, of course, she knows and has done so from the very first. I asked him once why he had never told her what it was that brought him so regularly to look at the peaches.

"And he said, in his quick, sharp way, 'Miss

Anthea, can't be done, Mam. A poor, battered old soldier—only one arm—no, Mam!'"

"I wonder if one could find just such another Sergeant outside Arcadia," said Bellew. "I wonder!"

Now they were approaching a stile, towards which Bellew had directed his eyes from time to time, as for that matter, curiously enough, had Anthea; but to him it seemed that it never would be reached, while to her it seemed that it would be reached much too soon.

Therefore, she began to rack her mind, trying to remember any gate or gap in the hedge that would obviate the necessity of crossing the stile.

But, before she could recall any such gate or gap, they were at the stile, and Bellew, vaulting over, had set down the basket and stretched out his hand to aid her.

Anthea, tall and lithe, active and vigorous with her outdoor life, and used to such things from her infancy, stood for a moment, hesitating.

To be sure, the stile was rather high; yet she could have vaulted it nearly, if not quite, as easily as Bellew himself, had she been alone. But then, she was not alone; moreover, be it remembered, this was in Arcadia, of a midsummer night.

So she hesitated, only for a moment, it is true, and then, seeing the quizzical look in his eyes that always made her vaguely rebellious, with a quick, light movement she mounted the stile, and there paused to shake her head in laughing disdain of his outstretched hand.

Then—there was the sound of rending cambric and she tripped, and the next moment he had caught her in his arms.

It was for but a very brief instant that she lay, soft and yielding, in his embrace, yet she could not but be conscious of how strong were the arms that held her so easily, before they set her down.

"I beg your pardon. How awkward I am!" she exclaimed, in her mortification.

"No," said Bellew, shaking his head. "It was a nail, you know, a bent and rusty nail—here, under the top bar. Is your dress torn much?"

"Oh, that is nothing, thank you!"

They went on again; but now they were silent once more, and very naturally, for Anthea was mightily angry with herself, the stile, and Bellew, and everything concerned, while he was thinking of the sudden, warm clasp of her arms, of the alluring fragrance of her hair, and of the shy droop of her lashes as she had lain in his embrace.

Therefore, as he walked on beside her, saying nothing, within his secret soul he poured benedictions upon the head of that bent and rusty nail.

Presently, having turned down a grassy lane and crossed a small but very noisy brook, they eventually came upon a small and very lonely little cottage.

Anthea paused, looking at Bellew with a dubious brow.

"I ought to warn you that Mrs. Dibbin is very old, and sometimes a little queer, and sometimes says very surprising things."

"Excellent," said Bellew, holding the little gate open for her. "Very right and proper conduct in a witch, and I love surprises above all things."

But Anthea still hesitated, while Bellew stood with his hand upon the gate, waiting for her to enter.

Now, he had left his hat behind him, and as the moon shone down on his bare head, she could not but notice how bright and yellow his hair was, despite the thick, black brows below.

"I think I . . . would rather you waited outside, if you don't mind, Mr. Bellew."

"You mean that I am to be denied the joy of conversing with a real, live old witch, and having my fortune told?"

He sighed.

"Well, if such is your will—so be it," he said, obediently, and handed her the basket.

"I won't keep you waiting very long, and . . . thank you," she said with a smile, and, hurrying up the narrow path, she tapped at the cottage door.

"Come in! come in!" cried an old, quivering voice. "That be my own soft dove of a maid, my proud, beautiful white lady! Come in, come in! And bring him with you, him as is so big, and strong, him as I've expected so long.

"The tall, golden man from over the seas. Bid him come in, Miss Anthea, that Goody Dibbin's old eyes may look on him at last."

Hereupon, at a sign from Anthea, Bellew turned in at the gate, strode up the path, and entered the cottage.

Despite the season, a fire burnt upon the hearth, and crouched over this, in a great elbow-chair, sat a very bent and aged woman.

She sat for a while, staring up at Bellew, who stood, tall and bare-headed, smiling down at her; and then all at once she nodded her head.

"Right," she said in a quavering voice, "right, right; it be all right! The golden man as I've watched this many an' many a day, wi' the curly hair and the sleepy eye, and the Tiger-mark upon his arm. Right! Right!"

"What do you mean by 'Tiger-mark'?" enquired Bellew.

"I mean, young master wi' your golden curls, I mean, as sitting here day in and day out, staring down into my fire, I had my dreams—leastways, I calls 'em my dreams, though there's them as calls it the 'second sight.'

"But pray sit down, tall Sir, on the stool there; and you, my tender maid, my dark lady, come you here, upon my right, and if you wish I'll look into the ink, or read your pretty hand, or tell you what I see down there in the fire.

"Ah, my proud lady, happy the man who shall win ye! Happy the man who shall wed ye, my dark, beautiful maid. And strong must be he, yes, and masterful, who shall wake the love-light in those great, passionate eyes of yours.

"And there is no man in all this world can do it, but he must be a golden man, wi' the Tiger-mark upon him."

"Why! Oh, Nannie. . . !"

"Ay, blush if ye will, my dark lady; but Mother Dibbin knows, she's seen it in the fire, dreamt it in her dreams, and read it in the ink. The path lies very dark afore ye, my lady, yes very dark it be, and full o' cares and troubles; but there's the sun shining beyond, bright and golden.

"You be proud and high, and scornful, my lady, 'tis in your blood. You'll need a strong hand to guide ye, and the strong hand shall come. By

force you shall be wooed, and by force you shall
be wed.

"And there be no man strong enough to woo
and wed ye, but him as I've told ye of, him as
bears the Tiger-mark."

"But, Nannie," said Anthea again, gently in-
terrupting her, and patting the old woman's
shrivelled hand, "you're forgetting the basket. You
haven't found what we've brought you yet."

"Yes, yes!" said old Nannie, nodding. "God
bless you, my sweet maid, for your kindly
thought."

And with a sudden gesture she caught Anthea's hand to her lips, and then, just as suddenly,
turned upon Bellew.

"And now, tall Sir, can I do ought for ye?
Shall I look into the fire for ye, or the ink, or read
your hand?"

"Why, yes," answered Bellew, stretching out
his hand to her. "You shall tell me two things, if
you will. First, shall one ever find his way into the
'Castle of Heart's Desire,' and secondly, when?"

"Oh, but I don't need to look into your hand
to tell you that, tall Sir; nor yet in the ink, or in
the fire, for I've dreamt it all in my dreams.

"And now, see you, 'tis a strong place, this
castle, wi' thick doors, and great locks, and bars.
But I have seen those doors broke down, those
great locks and bars burst asunder; but there is
none can do this but him as bears the Tiger-mark.

"So much for the first. And, for the second,
happiness shall come a-riding to you on the full
moon; but you must reach up and take it for yourself, if you be tall enough."

"And even you are not tall enough to do that,

Mr. Bellew," said Anthea, laughing, as she rose to bid old Nannie good-night, while Bellew, unnoticed, slipped certain coins upon a corner of the chimney-piece.

"At the full o' the moon, tall Sir," repeated old Nannie; "at the full o' the moon! As for you, my dark-eyed lady, I say by force you shall be wooed, and by force ye shall be wed. Yes, yes!

"But there is no man strong enough except he that has the Tiger-Mark upon him. Old Nannie knows. She's seen it in the ink, dreamt it in my dreams, and read it all in your pretty hand."

"Poor old Nannie!" said Anthea, as they went on down the grassy lane. "She is so very grateful for so little. And she is such a gentle creature really, though the country folk call her a witch and are afraid of her because they say she has the 'evil eye,' which is ridiculous of course! But nobody ever goes near her, and she is dreadfully lonely, poor old thing!"

"And that is why you come to sit with her and let her talk to you?" Bellew enquired, staring up at the moon.

"Yes."

"And do you believe in her dreams and visions?"

"No, of course not," answered Anthea, rather hurriedly, and with a deeper colour in her cheeks, though Bellew was still intent upon the moon. "You don't either, do you?"

"Well, I don't quite know," he answered slowly; "she is rather a wonderful old lady, I think."

"Yes, she has wonderfully thick hair still," said Anthea, "and she's not a bit deaf, and her eyes are as clear and sharp as ever they were."

"Yes, but I wasn't meaning her eyes, or her hair, or her hearing."

"Oh, then pray, what did you mean?"

"Did you happen to notice what she said about a—er—man with a Tiger-mark?" enquired Bellew, still gazing up at the moon.

"The man with the Tiger-mark!" Anthea laughed. "Of course! He has been much in her dreams lately, and she has talked of him a great deal."

"Has she?" said Bellew.

"Yes; her mind is full of strange twists and fancies. You see, she is so very old, and she loves to tell me her dreams and read the future for me."

"Though, of course, you don't believe it," said Bellew, questioningly.

"Believe it!" Anthea repeated, and walked some dozen paces or so, before she answered, "No, of course not."

"Then none of your fortune—nothing she told you—has ever come true?"

Once more Anthea hesitated, this time for so long that Bellew turned from his moon-gazing to look at her.

"I mean," he went on, "has none of it ever come true? About this man with the Tiger-mark, for instance?"

"No, oh no!" answered Anthea, rather hastily, and laughed again. "Old Nannie has seen him in her dreams . . . in India, and Africa, and China; in hot countries and cold countries.

"Oh, Nannie has seen him everywhere, but I have seen him nowhere, and of course I never shall."

"Ah," said Bellew. "And she reads him always in your fortune, does she?"

"And I listen very patiently," said Anthea, nodding, "because it pleases her so much; and it is all so very harmless, after all, isn't it?"

"Yes," answered Bellew, "and very wonderful."

"Wonderful? Poor old Nannie's fancies! What do you mean by 'wonderful'?"

"Upon my word, I hardly know," said Bellew, shaking his head. "But 'there are more things in heaven and earth,' etcetera, you know, and this is one of them."

"Really? Now you grow mysterious, Mr. Bellew."

"Like the night," he answered, turning to aid her across the brook.

"What did you mean when you said old Nannie's dreams were so wonderful?" Anthea asked after a moment.

"I'll show you," he answered.

While he spoke, he slipped off his coat and, drawing up his shirt-sleeve, held out a muscular, white arm towards her. He held it out in the full radiance of the moon, and thus, looking down at it, her eyes grew suddenly wide, and her breath caught strangely, as surprise gave place to something else.

For there, plain to be seen upon the white flesh, were three long scars that wound up from elbow to shoulder. And so, for a while, they stood thus, she looking at his arm, and he at her.

"Why," she said at last, finding her voice with a little gasp, "why, then . . ."

"I am the man with the Tiger-Mark," he said, smiling his slow, placid smile. "I got it in India."

Now, as his eyes looked down into hers, she

flushed sudden and hot, and her glance wavered, and fell beneath his.

"Oh," she cried; and with the word, turned about and fled from him into the house.

* * *

"Uncle Porges, there's a little man in the hall with a red, red nose, and a blue, blue chin . . ."

"Yes, I've seen him, also his nose and chin, my Porges."

"But he's sticking little papers with numbers on them all over my Auntie Anthea's chairs an' tables. Now, what do you s'pose he's doing that for?"

"Who knows? It's probably all on account of his red nose and blue chin, my Porges. Anyway, don't worry about him—let us, rather, find Auntie Anthea."

They found her in the hall. A hall that, years and years ago, had often rung with the clash of men-at-arms, and echoed with loud and jovial laughter, for this was the most ancient part of the Manor.

It looked rather bare and barren just now, for the furniture was all moved out of place, ranged neatly round the walls and stacked at the farther end, beneath the gallery, where the little man in question, blue of chin and red of nose, was hovering about it, dabbing little tickets on chairs and tables.

And, in the midst of it all, stood Anthea. A desolate figure, Bellew thought, who, upon his entrance, bent her head to draw on her driving-gloves, for she was waiting for the dog-cart, which was to bear her and Small Porges to Cranbrook, far away from the hollow tap of the auctioneer's hammer.

"We're getting rid of some of the old furniture, you see, Mr. Bellew," she said, laying her hand on an antique cabinet near-by. "We really have much more than we ever use."

"Yes," Bellew answered.

But he noticed that her eyes were very dark and wistful, despite her light tone, and that she had laid her hand upon the old cabinet with a touch very like a caress.

"Why is that man's nose so awful red and his chin so blue, Auntie Anthea?" enquired Small Porges, in a hissing stage-whisper.

"Hush, Georgy! I don't know," said Anthea.

"An' why is he sticking his little numbers all over our best furniture?"

"That is to guide the auctioneer."

"Where to? An' what's an auctioneer?"

But at this moment, hearing the wheels of the dog-cart at the door, Anthea turned and hastened out into the sunshine.

"A lovely day it do be for drivin'," said Adam, touching his hat. "An' Bess be thinkin' the same, I do believe."

Lightly and numbly Anthea swung herself up to the high seat, turning to make Small Porges secure beside her, as Bellew handed him up.

"You'll look after things for me, Adam?" asked Anthea, glancing back wistfully into the dim recesses of the cool, old hall.

"Yes, I will that, Miss Anthea."

"Mr. Bellew, we can find room for you, if you care to come with us."

"Thanks," he replied, shaking his head, "but

I rather think I'll stay here, and—er—help Adam to—to—look after things, if you don't mind."

"Then good-bye." And, nodding to Adam, she gave the mare her head, and off they went.

"Good-bye!" cried Small Porges. "An' thank you for the shilling, Uncle Porges!"

"The mare is—er—rather fresh this morning, isn't she, Adam?" enquired Bellew, watching the dog-cart's rapid course.

"Fresh, Sir!"

"And that's rather a—er—dangerous sort of thing for a woman to drive, isn't it?"

"Meaning the dog-cart, Sir?"

"Meaning the dog-cart, Adam."

"Why, Lord love ye, Mr. Belloo, Sir!" cried Adam, with his great laugh. "There ain't nobody can 'andle the ribbons better than Miss Anthea. There ain't a horse as she can't drive—ah, or ride, for that matter—not nowhere, Sir!"

"Hum!" And, having watched the dog-cart out of sight, he turned and followed Adam into the stables.

And here, sitting upon a bale of hay, they smoked many pipes together in earnest converse, until such time as the sale should begin.

As the day advanced, people began arriving in twos and threes, and amongst the first, the auctioneer himself.

Conspicuous amongst them was a large man with a fat, red neck, which he was continually mopping at, and rubbing with a vivid bandanna handkerchief, scarcely less red.

His voice, like himself, was large, with a peculiar brassy ring to it that penetrated to the farthest corners and recesses of the old hall.

He was, beyond all doubt, a man of substance, and of no small importance, for he was greeted deferentially on all hands, and it was to be noticed that people elbowed to each other to make way for him, as people ever will before substance and property.

Between whiles, however, he bestowed his undivided attention upon the furniture.

Bellew, watching all this from where he sat, screened from the throng by a great carved sideboard and divers chairs and what-nots, drew rather harder at his pipe, and, chancing to catch Adam's eye, beckoned him to approach.

"Who is that round, red man over there, Adam?" he enquired.

"That," replied Adam, in a tone of profound disgust, "that be Mr. Grimes, o' Cranbrook, Sir. Calls hisself a corn-chandler; but I calls 'im—well, never mind what, Sir! Only it weren't at corn-chandling as 'e made all 'is money, Sir. And it be him as we all work and slave for—here at Dapplemere Farm."

"What do you mean, Adam?"

"I mean as it be him as holds the mortgage on Dapplemere Farm, Sir."

"Ah! And for how much?"

"Over three thousand pound, Mr. Belloo, Sir!" Adam sighed, with a hopeless shake of the head. "An' that be a powerful lot o' money, Sir!"

Bellew thought of the sums he had lavished upon his yacht, upon his three racing-cars, and upon certain other extravagances.

Three thousand pounds—fifteen thousand dollars! It would make her a free woman—independent, happy! Just fifteen thousand dollars!

And he had thrown away more than that upon a poker-game before now!

At last the sale began, and, as Bellew had instructed, Adam began bidding.

"Twenty-five shillings," said Adam.

"At twenty-five shillings!" cried the auctioneer. "Any advance? A genuine, hand-painted, antique screen. Going at twenty-five—at twenty-five—going—going—gone! To the large gentleman in the neck-cloth, Theodore."

"Theer be that Job Jagway, Sir," said Adam, leaning across the sideboard to impart this information. "Over yonder, Mr. Belloo, Sir. Him as was bidding for the screen—the tall chap wi' the patches."

"The next lot I'm going to dispose of, gentlemen," the auctioneer went on, "is a fine set of six chairs, with carved antique backs, and upholstered in tapestry. Also, two arm-chairs to match. Wheel 'em out, Theodore. Now, what is your price for these eight fine pieces? Look 'em over and bid accordingly."

"Three pound!" said the fiery-necked cornchandler.

"Guineas," said another.

"Four pounds," said the corn-chandler.

"Four pound ten!" roared Adam.

"Five!" called Grimes, edging away from Adam's elbow.

"Six pound ten!" cried Adam.

"Seven!" from another corner of the room.

"Eight!" said Grimes.

"Ten!" roared Adam, growing desperate.

"Eleven!" said Grimes, beginning to mop at his neck again.

Adam hesitated. Eleven pounds seemed so

very much for those chairs that he had seen Prudence and the rosy-cheeked maids dust regularly every morning.

But then—it was not his money, after all. Therefore, Adam hesitated, and glanced wistfully towards a certain distant corner.

"At eleven—at eleven pounds! This fine suite of hand-carved antique chairs! At eleven pounds! At eleven! At eleven! Going—going . . ."

"Fifteen!" said a voice from the distant corner.

Whereupon Adam drew a great sigh of relief, while the corn-chandler contorted himself in his efforts to glare at Bellew round the sideboard.

"Fifteen pounds!" chanted the auctioneer. "I have fifteen—I am given fifteen. Any advance? These eight antique chairs, going! For the last time—going—gone! Sold to the gentleman in the corner, behind the sideboard, Theodore."

And so it went on, with Bellew now doing the bidding, until it came to the old sideboard.

"Any advance on eighty-five?" asked the auctioneer.

"Eighty-six," said Bellew, settling the tobacco in his pipe-bowl with his thumb.

Once again the auctioneer leant over and appealed to the corn-chandler, who stood in the same attitude, jingling the money in his pocket.

"Come, Sir. Don't let a pound or so stand between you and a sideboard that can't be matched in the length and breadth of the United Kingdom. Come, what do you say to another ten shillings?"

"I say, Sir," said Grimes, with his gaze still riveted upon Bellew, "I say—no, Sir. I say make it another twenty pounds, Sir!"

"One hundred and six pounds!" cried the auctioneer. "At one-six—at one-six!"

Bellew struck a match, but the wind from the open casement behind him extinguished it.

"I have one hundred and six pounds! Is there any advance? Yes or no? Going at one hundred and six!"

Adam, who up till now had enjoyed the struggle to the uttermost, experienced a sudden qualm of fear. Bellew struck another match.

"At one hundred and six pounds, at one-six —going at one hundred and six pounds!"

A cold moisture started out on Adam's brow. He clenched his hands and muttered between his teeth. Supposing the money were all gone, like his own share!

Supposing they had to lose this famous old sideboard—and to Grimes, of all people! This, and much more, was in Adam's mind while the auctioneer held his hammer poised, and Bellew went on lighting his pipe.

"Going at one hundred and six—going—going . . ."

"Fifty up!" said Bellew.

His pipe was well alight at last, and he was nodding to the auctioneer through a fragrant cloud.

"What?" cried Grimes. " 'Ow much?"

"Gent in the corner gives me one hundred and fifty-six pounds," said the auctioneer, with a jovial eye upon the corn-chandler's lowering visage. "One-five-six—all done—any advance? Going at one-five-six—going—going—gone!"

The hammer fell, and with its tap a sudden silence came upon the old hall. Then, all at once, the corn-chandler turned, caught up his hat, clapped it on, shook a fat fist at Bellew, and, crossing to the door, lumbered away, muttering maledictions as he went.

By twos and threes the others followed him, until there remained only Adam, Bellew, the auctioneer, and the red-nosed Theodore.

And yet there was one other, for, chancing to raise his eyes to the Minstrel's Gallery, Bellew saw Miss Priscilla, who, meeting his smiling glance, leant down suddenly over the curved rail and very deliberately threw him a kiss, and so hurried away with a quick, light tap-tap of her stick.

"Lord!" said Adam, pausing with a chair under either arm. "Lord, Mr. Bellew, Sir, I wonder what Miss Anthea will say?"

"Ah!" Bellew nodded thoughtfully. "I wonder!"

"What do you suppose she'll say, Miss Priscilla, Mam?" Adam asked as she came into the hall.

"I think you'd better be careful of that picture, Adam."

"Which means," said Bellew, smiling down into Miss Priscilla's young, bright eyes, "that you don't know."

"Well, Mr. Bellew, she'll be very glad, of course, happier, I think, than you or I can guess, because I know she loves every stick and stave of that old furniture. But . . ."

"But," Bellew nodded, "yes, I understand."

"Mr. Bellew, if Anthea, God bless her dear heart, but if she has a fault, it is pride, Mr. Bellew. Pride! Pride! Pride, with a capital P!"

"Yes, she is very proud."

"She'll be that 'appy-'earted," said Adam,

pausing near-by, with a great armful of miscellaneous articles, "an' that full o' joy as never was, Mr. Bellew, Sir!"

Having delivered himself of which, he departed with his load.

"I rose this morning very early, Mr. Bellew— oh, very early," said Miss Priscilla, following Adam's laden figure with watchful eyes. "Couldn't possibly sleep, you see. So I got up, ridiculously early; but, bless you, she was before me."

"Ah!"

"Oh dear, yes. Had been up hours! And what . . . what do you suppose she was doing?"

Bellew shook his head.

"She was rubbing and polishing that old sideboard that you paid such a dreadful price for . . . down on her knees before it. Yes, she was, and polishing and rubbing, and crying all the while!

"Oh, dear heart! Such great big tears, and so very quiet. When she heard my little stick come tapping along, she tried to hide them, and when I drew her dear, beautiful head down into my arms, she tried to smile.

"'I'm so very silly, Aunt Priscilla,' she said, crying more than ever; 'but it is so hard to let the old things be taken away. You see, I love them so!'

"I tell you all this, Mr. Bellew, because I like you, and secondly, I tell you all this to explain why I . . . hm . . ."

"Threw a kiss, from a Minstrel's Gallery, to a most unworthy individual, Aunt Priscilla!"

"Threw you a kiss, Mr. Bellew. I had to—the sideboard, you know . . . on her knees. You understand?"

"I understand."

"You see, Mr. Belloo, Sir," said Adam, at this juncture, speaking from beneath an inlaid table which he held balanced upon his head, "it ain't as if this was jest ordinary furniture, Sir. You see, she kinder feels as it be all part o' Dapplemere Manor, as it used to be called.

"It's all been here so long that them cheers an' tables has come to be part o' the 'ouse, Sir. So when she comes an' finds as it ain't all been took ... or, as you might say, vanished away ... why, the question as I asks you is ... wot will she say? Oh, Lord!"

When the hall was once more its old familiar, comfortable self, and the floor had been swept of its litter and every trace of the sale had been removed, Miss Priscilla sighed, and Bellew put on his coat.

"When do you expect she will come home?" he enquired, glancing at the grandfather-clock in the corner.

"Well, if she drove straight back from Cranbrook, she would be here now; but I fancy she won't be so very anxious to get home today, and may come the longest way round. Yes, it's in my mind she will keep away from Dapplemere as long as ever she can."

"And I think," said Bellew, "yes, I think I'll take a walk. I'll go and call upon the Sergeant."

"The Sergeant," said Miss Priscilla. "Let me see, it is now a quarter to five, and it should take you about fifteen minutes to the village, which will make it exactly five o'clock. You will find the Sergeant at the King's Head, you know.

"Not that I have ever seen him there, good gracious no! But I happen to be acquainted with his habits, and he is as regular and precise as his great big silver watch, and that is the most precise and regular thing in all the world.

"I am glad you are going," she went on, "because today is . . . well, a day apart, Mr. Bellew. You will find the Sergeant at the King's Head until half-past seven."

"Then I will go to the King's Head," said Bellew. "And what message do you send him?"

"None," replied Miss Priscilla, laughing and shaking her head. "At least, you can tell him, if you wish, that this evening the peaches are riper than ever they were."

"I won't forget," said Bellew, smiling, and went out into the sunshine.

But, crossing the yard, he was met by Adam, who, chuckling still, paused to touch his hat.

"To look at that theer 'all, Sir, you wouldn't never know as there'd ever been any sale at all— not no'ow. Now, the only question as worries me, and as I'm asking of myself constant, is—what will Miss Anthea have to say about it?"

"Yes," said Bellew. "I wonder!"

And so he turned and went away slowly across the fields.

Miss Priscilla had been right. Anthea was coming back the longest way round, for she was anxious to keep away from Dapplemere as long as possible.

Therefore, despite Small Porges' exhortations, and Bess's champing impatience, she held the mare in, permitting her only the slowest of paces, which was a most unusual thing for Anthea to do.

For the most part, too, she drove in silence, seemingly deaf to Small Porges' flow of talk, which was also very unlike her. But before her eyes were visions of her dismantled home, and in her ears was the roar of the voices clamouring for her cherished possessions—a sickening roar, broken now and then by the hollow tap of the auctioneer's cruel hammer!

But, slowly as they went, they came within sight of the house at last, with its quaint gables and many latticed windows and the blue smoke curling up from its twisted chimneys—smiling and placid, as though, in all this great world, there was no such thing to be found as an auctioneer's hammer.

Presently they swung into the drive and drew up in the courtyard. And there was Adam, waiting to take the mare's head. Adam, as good-natured and stolid as though there were no abominations called, for want of a worse name, sales.

Very slowly for her, Anthea climbed down from the high dog-cart, aiding Small Porges to earth, and with his hand clasped tight in hers, and with lips set firm, she turned and entered the hall.

But upon the threshold she stopped, and stood there utterly still, gazing upon the trim orderliness of everything.

Then, seeing every well-remembered possession in its appointed place, all things became suddenly blurred and dim, and, snatching her hand from Small Porges' clasp, she uttered a great, choking sob and covered her face.

But Small Porges had seen, and stood aghast, and Miss Priscilla had seen, and now hurried forward with a quick tap-tap of her stick.

As she came, Anthea raised her head and looked for one who should have been there but was not.

And in that moment, instinctively she knew

how things came to be as they were, and because of this knowledge, her cheeks flamed with a swift, burning colour, and with a soft cry she hid her face in Miss Priscilla's gentle bosom.

Then, while her face was yet hidden there, she whispered:

"Tell me . . . tell me . . . all about it."

But meanwhile Bellew, striding far away across the meadows, seeming to watch the glory of the sunset, and to hearken to a blackbird piping from the dim seclusion of the copse a melodious good-bye to the dying day, yet saw and heard it not at all, for his mind was still occupied with Adam's question:

"What will Miss Anthea say?"

Chapter Four

Before Bellew reached the Inn he saw a small crowd gathered about a trap, in which sat two men, one of whom he recognised as the red-necked corn-chandler, Grimes, and the other, his assistant, Parsons.

The corn-chandler was mopping violently at his face and neck, down which ran, and to which clung, a foamy substance suspiciously like the froth of beer, and as he mopped, his loud, brassy voice shook and quivered with passion.

"I tell ye—you shall get out o' my cottage!" he was saying. "I say you shall quit my cottage at the end o' the month—and when I says a thing, I means it.

"I say you shall get off o' my property—you, and that beggarly cobbler. I say you shall be throwed out o' my cottage—lock, stock, and barrel. I say . . ."

"I wouldn't, Mr. Grimes—leastways, not if I was you," another voice broke in, calm and deliberate. "No, I wouldn't say another word, Sir; because, if you do say another word, I know a man as will drag you down out o' that cart, Sir.

"I know a man as will break your whip over your very own back, Sir. I know a man as will then take and heave you into the horse-pond, Sir. And that man is me—Sergeant Appleby, late of the Nineteenth Hussars, Sir!"

The corn-chandler, having removed most of the froth from his head and face, stared down at the straight, alert figure of the big Sergeant, hesitated, glanced at the Sergeant's fist, which, though solitary, was large and powerful, and scowled.

Snatching his whip, he cut viciously at his horse, very much as if that animal had been the Sergeant himself, and as the trap lurched forward, he shook his fist and nodded his head.

"Out ye go at the end o' the month—mind that," he said with a snarl, and so rattled away down the road, still mopping at his head and neck, until he had fairly mopped himself out of sight.

"Well, Sergeant," said Bellew, extending his hand, "how are you?"

"Hearty, Sir, I thank you. Though at this precise moment, just a little put out, Sir. Nonetheless, I am happy to see you, Mr. Bellew, Sir."

He smiled at Bellew before he went on:

"My cottage lies down the road, yonder, an easy march. If you will step that far—speaking for my comrade and myself—we shall be proud for you to take tea with us."

"Thank you very much."

"You will be wondering at the tantrums of the man Grimes, Sir, of his ordering me and my comrade Peterday out of his cottage," the Sergeant explained as they walked down the road.

"I'll tell you in two words. It's all owing to

the sale—up at the farm. You see, Grimes is a great hand at buying things uncommonly cheap, and selling 'em uncommonly dear. Today, it seems, he was disappointed."

"Ah!" said Bellew.

"I were sitting in my usual corner when in comes Grimes, like a thunder-cloud. Calls for a pint of ale, in a tankard. Tom, the landlord, draws a pint.

" 'Buy anything at the sale, Mr. Grimes?' he says.

" 'Sale!' says Grimes. 'Sale, indeed!' And then he falls a-cursing folk up at the farm—shocking —outrageous. Ends by threatening to foreclose mortgage—within the month.

"Upon which I raise a protest, upon which he grows abusive, upon which I was forced to pour his ale over him—after which I ran him out into the road. And there it is, you see."

"And he threatened to foreclose the mortgage on Dapplemere Farm, did he, Sergeant?"

"Within the month, Sir! Upon which I warned him—Inn parlour, no place—lady's private money troubles—gaping crowd—dammit!"

"And so he is turning you out of his cottage?"

"Within the week, Sir. But then, beer down the neck is rather unpleasant!"

He uttered a short laugh, then was immediately grave again.

"It isn't," he went on, "it isn't as I mind the ill-convenience of moving, Sir—though I shall be mighty sorry to leave the old place, but there's my comrade, Peterday. He is a remarkable man— most cobblers are. He lost his leg in a gale of wind off the Cape of Good Hope—for my comrade was a sailor, Sir.

"Consequently he is a handy man, and makes his own wooden legs, Sir—and here we are."

Saying which, the Sergeant halted, wheeled, opened a very small gate, and ushered Bellew into a very small garden, bright with flowers, beyond which was a very small cottage indeed.

"Peterday," said the Sergeant, "Mr. Bellew."

"Glad to see you, Sir," said the mariner, saluting the visitor with a quick bob of the head, and a backwards scrape of the wooden leg. "You couldn't make port at a better time, Sir, and because why? Because the kettle's a-boiling, Sir, the muffins is piping-hot, and the shrimps is a-laying hove, too, waiting to be taken aboard."

"Mr. Bellew, Sir," the Sergeant said, when they had finished tea, "this evening being the anniversary of a certain event, Sir, I will ask you to excuse me while I make the necessary preparations to honour this anniversary, as is ever my custom."

"A fine fellow is Dick, Sir!" said Peterday, beginning to fill a long clay pipe. "And tonight he goes on guard according to custom."

"On guard," repeated Bellew; "I'm afraid I don't understand."

"Of course you don't, Sir," said Peterday, chuckling. "Well then, tonight he marches away in full regimentals to mount guard. And where do you suppose? Why, I'll tell you—under Miss Priscilla's window. It's her birthday, you see, Sir!

"He gets there as the clock is striking eleven, and there he stays, a-marching to and fro, until twelve o'clock. Which does him a world o' good, and noways displeases Miss Priscilla—because why?—because she don't know nothing whatever about it."

"Mr. Bellew and comrade," the Sergeant said, when he returned, giving them both a drink, "I would like to make a toast to Miss Priscilla."

"God bless her," said Peterday.

"Amen," added Bellew.

So the toast was drunk; then the glasses were emptied, refilled, and emptied again—this time more slowly—and, the clock striking nine, Bellew rose to take his leave. Seeing which, the Sergeant fetched his hat and stick and volunteered to accompany him a little way.

So when Bellew had shaken the honest sailor's hand, they set out together.

"Sergeant," said Bellew, after they had walked some distance, "I have a message for you."

"For me, Sir?"

"From Miss Priscilla."

"From—indeed, Sir!"

"She bade me tell you that the peaches are riper tonight than ever they were."

The Sergeant seemed to find this a subject for profound thought, and he strode on beside Bellew very silently, and with his eyes straight before him.

"That the peaches were riper—tonight—than ever they were," he said at last.

"Yes, Sergeant."

"Riper!" said the Sergeant, as though turning this over in his mind.

"Riper than ever they were," said Bellew, nodding.

"The peaches, I think, Sir?"

"The peaches, yes." Bellew heard the Sergeant's finger rasping to and fro across his shaved chin.

"Mr. Bellew, Sir, she is a very remarkable woman."

"Yes, Sergeant."

"A wonderful woman."

"Yes, Sergeant."

"The kind of woman that improves with age."

"Yes, Sergeant."

"Talking of peaches, I've often thought she is very like a peach herself."

"Very, Sergeant, but . . ."

"Well, Sir?"

"Peaches do not improve with age, Sergeant, and the peaches are riper than ever they were—tonight!"

The Sergeant stopped short and stared at Bellew wide-eyed.

"Why—Sir," he said very slowly, "you don't mean to say you think as she meant—that . . ."

"But I do!" said Bellew, nodding.

And now, just as suddenly as he had stopped, the Sergeant turned and went on again.

"Lord!" he whispered. "Lord! Lord!"

The moon was rising, and looking at the Sergeant, Bellew saw that there was a wonderful light in his face, yet a light that was not of the moon.

"Sergeant," said Bellew, laying a hand upon his shoulder, "why don't you speak to her?"

"Speak to her—what, me? No, no, Mr. Bellew!" said the Sergeant, hastily. "No, no—can't be done —not to be mentioned, or thought of!"

The light was all gone out of his face now, and he walked with his chin on his breast.

"The surprising thing to me, Sergeant, is that you have never thought of putting your fortune to the test, and—speaking your mind to her before now."

"Thought of it!" repeated the Sergeant bitterly. "Thought of it! Lord, Sir, I've thought of it these five years—and more, I've thought of it day and night—I've thought of it so very much that I know I never can speak my mind to her.

"Look at me!" he cried suddenly, wheeling and confronting Bellew, but not at all like his bold, erect, soldierly self. "Yes, look at me—a poor, battered, old soldier with his best arm gone —left behind him in India, and with nothing in the world but his old uniform.

"Look at me, with the best o' my days behind me, and wi' only one arm left—and I'm a deal more awkward and helpless with that one arm than you'd think; look at me, and then tell me how such a man could dare to speak his mind to such a woman.

"What right has such a man to even think of speaking his mind to such a woman, when there's part o' that man already in the grave?

"Why, no right, Sir, none in the world. Poverty and one arm are facts as make it impossible for that man to ever speak his mind. And, Sir—that man never will. Sir—good-night to you, and a pleasant walk—I turn back here."

Which the Sergeant did, then and there, wheeling sharply about-face; yet, as Bellew watched him go, he noticed that the soldier's step was heavy and slow, and it seemed that, for once, the Sergeant had even forgotten to put on his imaginary spurs.

* * *

"Adam!"
"Yes, Miss Anthea?"

"How much money did Mr. Bellew give you to buy the furniture?"

Adam twisted his hat in his hand and stared at the ceiling, and the floor, and the table before Miss Anthea, and the wall behind Miss Anthea—anywhere but at Miss Anthea.

"You ask me—how much it were, Miss Anthea?"

"Yes, Adam."

"Well—it were a goodish sum."

"Was it . . . fifty pounds?"

"Fifty pound!" repeated Adam, in a tone of lofty disdain. "No, Miss Anthea, it were not fifty pound."

"Do you mean it was more?"

"Ah," said Adam, nodding, "I mean as it were a sight more. If you was to take the fifty pound you mention, add twenty more, and then another twenty to that, and then come ten more to that —why then, you'd be a bit nearer the figure . . ."

"A hundred pounds!" exclaimed Anthea, aghast.

"Ah, a hundred pound," said Adam, rolling the words upon his tongue with great gusto, "one hundred pound were the sum, Miss Anthea."

"Oh, Adam!"

"Lord love you, Miss Anthea, that weren't nothing—that were only a flea-bite, as you might say. He give more—ah, nigh double as much as that for the sideboard."

"Nonsense, Adam!"

"It be gospel true, Miss Anthea. That there sideboard were the plum o' the sale, so to speak, an' old Grimes had set 'is 'eart on it, ye see. Well, it were bid up to eighty-six pound, an' there old

Grimes 'e goes twenty more, making it a hundred an' six.

"Then, just as I thought it were all over, an just as that there old Grimes were beginning to swell himself wi' triumph, an' get that red in the face as 'e were a sight to behold—Mr. Belloo— who'd been lightin' 'is pipe all this time—up and says:

" 'Fifty up!' 'e says in his quiet way, making it a hundred an' fifty pound, Miss Anthea—which were too much for Grimes. Lord! I thought as that there man were going to burst, Miss Anthea!" Then Adam gave bent to his great laugh at the mere recollection.

But Anthea was grave enough, and the troubled look in her eyes quickly sobered him.

"A hundred and fifty-six pounds!" she repeated in an awed voice. "But it . . . it is awful!"

"Steepish," said Adam, nodding, "pretty steepish for a old sideboard, I'll allow, Miss Anthea—but you see, it were a personal matter between Grimes an' Mr. Belloo. I began to think as they never would have left off biddin'—an' by George! I don't believe as Mr. Belloo ever would have left off biddin'."

"But, Adam, why did he do it? Why did he buy all that furniture?"

"Well, to keep it from being took away, p'raps."

"Oh, Adam . . . what am I to do?"

"Do, Miss Anthea?"

"The mortgage must be paid off . . . dreadfully soon . . . you know that, and . . . I can't . . . oh, I can't give the money back . . ."

"What? Give it back? No, o' course not, Miss Anthea!"

"But I can't keep it."

"Can't keep it, Miss Anthea, Mam—an' why not?"

"Because I'm very sure he doesn't want all those things, the idea is quite . . . absurd! And yet . . . even if the hops do well, the money they bring will hardly be enough by itself, and so . . . I was selling my furniture to make it up, and . . . now . . . Oh, what am I to do?"

She leant her head wearily upon her hand.

Now, seeing her distress, Adam, all sturdy loyalty that he was, sighed in sympathy.

"Miss Anthea," he said, drawing a step nearer and lowering his voice mysteriously, "supposing as I was to tell you that 'e did want that furniture—ah, an' wanted it bad?"

"Now, how can he, Adam? It isn't as though he lived in England," said Anthea, shaking her head; "his home is thousands of miles away . . . he is an American, and besides . . ."

"Ah—but then, even a American may get married, Miss Anthea, Mam!"

"Married!" she repeated, glancing up very quickly. "Adam . . . what do you mean?"

"Why, you must know," began Adam, wringing at his hat again; "ever since the day I found him asleep in your hay, Miss Anthea, Mam, Mr. Belloo has been very kind and friendly-like.

"Mr. Belloo an' me have smoked a good many sociable pipes together, an' when men smoke together, Miss Anthea, they likewise talk together."

"Yes . . . well?" questioned Anthea, rather breathlessly, and took up a pencil that happened to be lying near to hand.

"And Mr. Belloo," continued Adam, heavily, "Mr. Belloo has done me—the—the honour,"

Adam paused to give an extra twist to his hat, "the honour, Miss Anthea . . ."

"Yes, Adam?"

"Of confiding to me 'is 'opes . . ." said Adam slowly, finding it much harder to frame his well-meaning falsehood than he had supposed.

"His h-o-p-e-s 'opes, Miss Anthea—of settling down very soon, an' of marryin' a fine lady as 'e 'as 'ad 'is eye on a goodish time, 'aving knowed her from childhood's hour, Miss Anthea, and as lives up to Lonnon . . ."

"Yes . . . Adam."

"Consequently, 'e bought all your furniture to set up 'ousekeepin', don't you see?"

"Yes . . . I see, Adam."

Her voice was low, soft and gentle as ever, but the pencil in her shaking fingers was tracing meaningless scrawls.

"So you don't 'ave to be no-wise backwards about keepin' the money, Miss Anthea."

"Oh, no . . . no, of course not. I . . . I understand, it was . . . just a . . . business transaction."

"Ah—that's it, a business transaction!" said Adam, nodding. "So you'll put the money to one side to help pay off the mortgage, eh, Miss Anthea?"

"Yes."

"If the 'ops come up to what they promise to come up to—you'll be able to get rid of old Grimes for good an' all, Miss Anthea."

"Yes, Adam."

"An' you be quite easy in your mind now, Miss Anthea, about keepin' the money?"

"Quite! Thank you, Adam . . . for . . . telling me. You can go now."

"Why then—good-night, Miss Anthea, Mam.

The mortgage is as good as paid—there ain't no such 'ops nowhere so good as ours be. An' you're quite free o' care, an' 'appy-'earted, Miss Anthea?"

"Quite . . . oh, quite, Adam!"

But when Adam's heavy tread had died away, when she was all alone, she behaved rather strangely for one so carefree and happy-hearted.

Something bright and glistening splashed upon the paper before her, the pencil slipped from her fingers, and with a sudden, choking cry she swayed forward and hid her face in her hands.

*   *   *

"To be or not to be."

Bellew leant against the mighty bole of "King Arthur" and stared up at the moon with knitted brows.

"That is the question! Whether I shall brave the slings and arrows and things, and speak tonight, and have done with it—one way or another, or live on awhile, secure in this uncertainty.

"To wait? Whether I shall, at this so early stage, pit all my chances of happiness against the chances of losing her—and with her, Small Porges, bless him, and all the quaint and lovable things of this wonderful Arcadia of mine.

"For, if her answer be 'no,' what recourse have I—what is there left me but to go wandering forth again, following the wind, and with the gates of Arcadia shut upon me forever?

" 'To be, or not to be'—that is the question!"

"Be that you, Mr. Belloo, Sir?"

"Even so, Adam. Come sit ye awhile, good

knave, and gaze upon Dian's loveliness, and smoke, and let us converse of dead kings."

"Why, kings ain't much in my line, Sir—living or dead uns—me never 'aving seen any—except a pic'ter—and that tore, though very life-like. But what I were a-lookin' for you for, was to ask you to back me up—an' to—play the game, Mr. Belloo, Sir."

"Why, as to that, my good Adam—my gentle Daphnis—my rugged Euphemio—you may rely upon me to the uttermost. Are you in trouble? Is it counsel you need, or only money?

"Fill your pipe, and while you smoke, confide your cares to me—put me wise, or as your French cousins would say—make me *au fait.*"

"Well," began Adam, when his pipe was well alight, "in the first place, Mr. Belloo, Sir, I begs to remind you as Miss Anthea sold her furniture to raise enough money, as with what the 'ops will bring, to pay off the mortgage—for good an' all."

"Yes."

"Well, tonight, Sir, Miss Anthea calls me into the parlour to ask—or, as you might say, enquire —as to the why an' likewise the wherefore of you a-buyin' all that furniture."

"Did she, Adam?"

"Ah! 'Why did 'e do it?' she says. 'Well, to keep it from bein' took away, p'raps,' says I— sharp as any gimblet, Sir."

"Good," said Bellew, nodding.

"Ah, but it weren't no good, Sir," returned Adam, "because she says as 'ow your 'ome being in America, you couldn't really need the furniture —nor yet want the furniture—an' blest if she wasn't talkin' of handing you the money back again."

"Hm!" said Bellew.

"Seeing which, Sir, an' because she must have that money if she 'opes to keep the roof of Dapplemere over 'er head, I, there an' then, made up or as you might say concocted a story, a anecdote, or a yarn—upon the spot, Mr. Belloo, Sir."

"Most excellent, Machiavelli! Proceed."

"I told her, Sir, as you bought that furniture on account of you being wishful to settle down; whereat she starts, an' looks at me wi' her eyes big, all surprised-like.

"I told 'er likewise, as you had told me on the quiet—or, you might say, confidential—that you bought that furniture to set up 'ousekeeping on account o' you being on the point o' marryin' a fine young lady up to Lonnon . . ."

"What!"

Bellew didn't move, nor did he raise his voice; nevertheless, Adam started back and instinctively threw up his arm.

"You told her that?"

"I did, Sir."

"But you knew it was a confounded lie!"

"Ay—I knowed it. But I'd tell a hundred— ah! thousands o' lies—confounded or otherwise— to save Miss Anthea."

"To save her?"

"From ruination, Sir! From losing Dapplemere Farm an' everything she has in the world. Lord love ye—the 'ops can never bring in by theirselves all the three thousand pound as is owing—it ain't to be expected.

"But if that three thousand pound ain't paid over to that dirty Grimes by next Saturday, that dirty Grimes turns Miss Anthea out o' Dapplemere, wi' Master Georgy an' poor little Miss Priscilla.

"An' what'll become o' them then—I don't know. Lord! When I think of it the 'Old Adam' do rise up in me to that extent as I'm minded to take a pitchfork and go and skewer that there Grimes to his own chimney corner.

"Ye see, Mr. Belloo, Sir," he went on, seeing that Bellew was still silent, "Miss Anthea be that proud, an' independent, that she'd never ha' took your money, Sir, if I hadn't told her that there lie —so that's why I did tell her that there lie."

"I see," Bellew nodded, "I see—yes—you did quite right. You acted for the best, and you did quite right, Adam, yes, quite right."

"Thankee, Sir."

"And so this is the game I am to play, is it?"

"That's it, Sir; if she asks you—are you goin' to get married, you'll tell her 'yes'—to a lady as you've knowed from your childhood's hour—living in Lonnon—that's all, Sir."

"That's all, is it, Adam?" said Bellew, slowly, turning to look up at the moon again. "It doesn't sound very much, does it? Well, I'll play your game, Adam—yes, you may depend upon me."

"Thankee, Mr. Belloo, Sir—thankee! Though I do 'ope as you'll excuse me for taking such liberties, an' making so free wi' your 'eart, and your affections, Sir!"

"Oh, certainly, Adam—the cause excuses— everything."

"Then, good-night, Sir."

"Good-night, Adam!"

So this good, well-meaning Adam strode

away, proud on the whole of his night's work, leaving Bellew to frown up at the moon with teeth clenched tight upon his pipe-stem.

Presently Bellew knocked the ashes from his pipe, and, rising, walked on slowly towards the house.

As he approached he heard someone playing the piano, and the music accorded well with his mood, or his mood with the music, for it was haunting, and very sweet, and with a recurring melody in a minor key that seemed to voice all the sorrows of humanity, past, present, and to come.

Drawn by the music, he crossed the rose-garden and, reaching the terrace, paused there, for the long French windows were open, and from where he stood he could see Anthea seated at the piano.

She was dressed in a white gown of some soft, clinging material, and amongst the heavy braids of her hair was a single great, red rose.

As he watched, he thought she had never looked more beautiful than now, with the soft glow of the candles upon her, for her face reflected the tender sadness of the music; it was in the mournful droop of her scarlet lips and the sombre depths of her eyes.

Close beside her sat little Miss Priscilla, busy with her needle, as usual; but now she paused and, lifting her head in her quick, bird-like way, looked up at Anthea, long and fixedly.

"Anthea, my dear," she said suddenly, "I'm fond of music, and I love to hear you play, as you know ... but I never heard you play quite so ... dolefully ... dear me, no ... that's not the right word, nor 'dismal' .... but I mean something between the two."

"I thought you were fond of Grieg, Aunt Priscilla."

"So I am, but then, even in his gayest moments, poor Mr. Grieg was always breaking his heart over something or other. And ... Gracious! There's Mr. Bellew at the window. Pray, come in, Mr. Bellew, and tell us how you liked Peterday, and the muffins!"

"Thank you," replied Bellew, stepping in through the long French window, "but I should like to hear Miss Anthea play again, first, if she will."

But Anthea, who had already risen from the piano, shook her head.

"I only play when I feel like it ... to please myself ... and Aunt Priscilla," she said, crossing to the broad, low window-seat and leaning out into the fragrant night.

"Why then," said Bellew, sinking into the easy-chair that Miss Priscilla indicated with a little stab of her needle, "why then, the muffins were delicious, Aunt Priscilla, and Peterday was just exactly what a one-legged mariner ought to be."

"And the shrimps, Mr. Bellew?" enquired Miss Priscilla, busy at her sewing again.

"Out-shrimped all other shrimps," he answered, glancing to where Anthea sat with her chin propped in her hand, gazing up at the waning moon, seemingly quite oblivious of him.

"And did he pour out the tea?" enquired Miss Priscilla, "from the china pot with the blue flowers, and the Chinese Mandarin fanning himself, and very awkward of course, with his one hand ... I don't mean the Mandarin, Mr. Bellew ... and very full of apologies?"

"He did."

"Just as usual; yes, he always does. And every year he gives me three lumps of sugar, and I only take one, you know. It's a pity," said Miss Priscilla, sighing, "that it was his right arm ... a great pity."

She sighed again, and, catching herself, glanced up quickly at Bellew, and smiled to see how completely absorbed he was in contemplation of the silent figure in the window-seat.

"But, after all, better a right arm than a leg," she pursued, "at least, I think so."

"Certainly," murmured Bellew.

"A man with only one leg, you see, would be almost as helpless as an old woman with a crippled foot ..."

"Who grows younger and brighter every year!" added Bellew, turning to her with his pleasant smile; "yes, and I think prettier."

"Oh, Mr. Bellew," exclaimed Miss Priscilla, shaking her head at him reprovingly, yet looking pleased nonetheless, "how can you be so ridiculous—good gracious me!"

"Why, it was the Sergeant who put it into my head."

"The Sergeant!"

"Yes, it was after I had given him your message about peaches, and ..."

"Oh, dear heart!" exclaimed Miss Priscilla at this juncture. "Prudence is out tonight, and I promised to bake the bread for her, and here I sit chatting and gossiping while that bread goes rising and rising all over the kitchen."

Miss Priscilla laid aside her sewing and, catching up her stick, hurried to the door.

"And I was almost forgetting to wish you 'many happy returns of the day,' Aunt Priscilla."

At this familiar appellation, Anthea turned sharply, in time to see him stoop and kiss Miss Priscilla's small white hand.

Then he opened the door, and Miss Priscilla tapped away, even more quickly than usual.

Anthea was half-sitting, half-kneeling amongst the cushions in the corner of the deep window-seat, apparently still lost in contemplation of the moon.

So much so that she did not stir, or even lower her upward gaze, when Bellew came and stood beside her. Therefore, taking advantage of the fixity of her regard, he once more became absorbed in her loveliness.

This was a most unwise procedure in Arcadia, by the light of a midsummer moon! And he mentally contrasted the dark, proud beauty of her face with those of all the other women he had ever known—to their utter and complete disparagement.

"Well?" enquired Anthea, at last, perfectly conscious of his look, and finding the silence growing irksome, yet still with her eyes averted. "Well, Mr. Bellew?"

"On the contrary," he answered, "the moon is on the wane."

"The moon!" she repeated. "Suppose it is . . . what then?"

"True happiness can only come riding astride the full moon, you know—you remember old Nannie told us so."

"And you . . . believed it?" she enquired scornfully.

"Why, of course," he answered in his quiet way.

Anthea didn't speak.

"And so," he went on, quite unabashed, "when I see happiness riding astride the full moon, I shall just reach up, in the most natural manner in the world, and take it down so that it may abide with me, world without end."

"Do you think you will be tall enough?"

"We shall see—when the time comes."

"I think it's all very ridiculous," said Anthea.

"Why then, suppose you play for me that same plaintive piece you were playing as I came in—something of Grieg's, I think it was. Will you, Miss Anthea?"

She was on the point of refusing, but then, as if moved by some capricious whim, she crossed to the piano and dashed into the riotous music of a Polish dance.

As the wild notes leapt beneath her quick, brown fingers, Bellew, seated near-by, kept his eyes upon the great red rose in her hair, which nodded slyly at him with her every movement.

Surely in all the world there had never bloomed a more tantalising, more wantonly provoking rose than this, wherefore Bellew, very wisely, turned his eyes from its glowing temptation.

Observing which, the rose, in evident desperation, nodded and swayed, until it had fairly nodded itself from its sweet resting-place and, falling to the floor, lay within Bellew's reach.

He promptly stooped and picked it up, and even as (with a last crashing chord) Anthea ceased playing and turned, in that same moment he dropped it deftly into his coat-pocket.

"Oh! By the way, Mr. Bellew," she said, speaking as if the idea had just entered her mind, "what do you intend to do about . . . all your furniture?"

"Do about it?" he repeated, settling the rose carefully in a corner of his pocket where it would not be crushed by his pipe.

"I mean ... where would you like it ... stored until you can send, and have it ... taken away?"

"Well, I—er—rather thought of keeping it where it is, if you don't mind."

"I'm afraid that will be ... impossible, Mr. Bellew."

"Why then, the barn will be an excellent place for it; I don't suppose the rats and mice will do it any real harm, and as for the damp, and the dust ..."

"Oh, you know what I mean!" exclaimed Anthea, beginning to tap the floor impatiently with her foot. "Of course we can't go on using the things now that they are your property; it ... wouldn't be ... right."

"Very well." He nodded, his fingers questing anxiously after the rose again. "I'll get Adam to help me shift it all into the barn tomorrow morning."

"Will you please be serious, Mr. Bellew?"

"As an owl," he said with a nod.

"Why then, of course, you will be leaving Dapplemere soon, and I should like to know exactly when, so that I can ... make the necessary arrangements."

"But you see, I am not leaving Dapplemere soon, or even thinking of it."

"Not?" she repeated, glancing up at him in swift surprise.

"Not until you bid me."

"I?"

"You!"

"But I . . . I understand that you . . . intend to . . . settle down."

"Certainly." Bellew nodded, transferring his pipe to another pocket altogether, lest it should damage the rose's tender petals. "To settle down has lately become the—er—ambition of my life."

"Then pray," said Anthea, taking up a sheet of music and beginning to study it with attentive eyes, "be so good as to tell me . . . what you mean."

"That necessarily brings us back to the moon again," answered Bellew.

"The moon?"

"The moon!"

"But what in the world has the moon to do with your furniture?" she demanded, her foot beginning to tap again.

"Everything—I bought that furniture with —er—with one eye on the moon, as it were—consequently the furniture, the moon, and I are indissolubly bound together."

"You are pleased to talk in riddles tonight, and really, Mr. Bellew, I have no time to waste over them, so if you will excuse me . . ."

"Thank you for playing for me," he said, as he held the door open for her.

"I played because I . . . felt like it, Mr. Bellew."

"Nevertheless, I thank you."

"When you make up your mind about . . . the furniture . . . please let me know."

"When the moon is at the full, yes."

"Can it be possible that you are still harping on the wild words of poor old Nannie?" she exclaimed.

"Nannie is very old, I'll admit," he said with a nod, "but surely you remember that we proved her right in one particular—I mean about the Tiger Mark, you know."

Now, when he said this, for no apparent reason the eyes that had been looking into his, proud and scornful, wavered, and were hidden under their long, thick lashes; the colour flamed in her cheeks, and without another word she was gone.

Bellew went outside again and sat beneath the shade of "King Arthur," alone with his thoughts.

Presently, however, he was surprised to hear the house door open, and close very softly, and to behold not the object of his meditations but Miss Priscilla coming towards him.

As she caught sight of him in the shadow of the tree, she stopped and stood leaning upon her stick as though she was rather disconcerted.

"Aunt Priscilla," he said, rising.

"Oh, it's you!" she exclaimed, just as though she hadn't known it all along. "Dear me, Mr. Bellew, how lonely you look, and dreadfully thoughtful, good gracious!"

She glanced up at him with her quick, girlish smile.

"I suppose you are wondering what I am doing out here at this unhallowed time of night—it must be nearly eleven o'clock. Oh dear me, yes, you are; well, sit down and I'll tell you. Let us sit here, in the darkest corner . . . there. Dear heart, how bright the moon is, to be sure."

So saying, Miss Priscilla ensconced herself at the very end of the rustic bench, where the deepest shadow lay.

"Well, Mr. Bellew," she began, "as you know, today is my birthday. As to my age, I am, let us say, just turned twenty-one; and, being young and foolish, Mr. Bellew, I have come out here to watch another very foolish person.

"A ridiculous old Sergeant of Hussars, who will come marching along very soon to mount guard in full regimentals, Mr. Bellew, with his busby on his head, with his braided tunic and dolman, and his great big boots, and with his spurs jingling, and his sabre bright under the moon."

"So, then, you know he comes?"

"Why, of course I do. And I love to hear the jingle of his spurs, and to watch the glitter of his sabre. So every year I come here and sit amongst the shadows, where he can't see me, and watch him go march, march, marching up and down and to and fro, until the clock strikes twelve, and he goes marching home again.

"Oh, dear me, it's all very foolish, of course, but I love to hear the jingle of his spurs."

"And have you sat here watching him every year?"

"Every year."

"And has he never guessed that you were watching him?"

"Good gracious me, of course not."

"Don't you think, Aunt Priscilla, that you are just a little—cruel?"

"Cruel . . . why . . . what do you mean?"

"I gave him your message, Aunt Priscilla."

"What message?"

"That 'tonight the peaches are riper than ever they were.'"

"Oh!" said Miss Priscilla, and waited expectantly for Bellew to continue.

But, as he was silent, she glanced at him, and seeing him staring at the moon, she looked at it also.

After she had gazed for perhaps half a minute, as Bellew was still silent, she spoke, though in
a very small voice indeed.

"And . . . what did . . . he say?"

"Who?" enquired Bellew.

"Why, the . . . Sergeant, to be sure."

"Well, he gave me to understand that a poor
old soldier, with only one arm left him, must be
content to stand aside always, and hold his peace,
just because he is a poor, maimed, old soldier.
Don't you think that you have been just a little
cruel all these years, Aunt Priscilla?"

"Sometimes . . . one is cruel . . . only to be . . .
kind!" she answered.

"Aren't the peaches ripe enough after all,
Aunt Priscilla?"

"Over-ripe," she said bitterly, "oh . . . they are
over-ripe."

"Is that all, Aunt Priscilla?"

"No," she answered, "no, there's . . . this!"
She held up her little crutch-stick.

"Is that all, Aunt Priscilla?"

"Oh . . . isn't . . . that enough?"

Bellew rose.

"Where are you going . . . what are you going
to do?" she demanded.

"Wait!" he said, smiling down at her perplex-
ity, and so he turned, and crossed to a certain corner of the orchard.

When he came back he held out a great glowing peach towards her.

"You are quite right," he said, nodding, "it
was so ripe that it fell at a touch."

As he spoke, she drew him down beside her in
the shadow.

"Hush!" she whispered. "Listen!"

Now as they sat there, very silent, faint and far away upon the still night air, they heard a sound—a silvery rhythmic sound it was, like the musical clash of fairy-cymbals, which drew rapidly nearer and nearer.

Bellew felt Miss Priscilla's hand trembling upon his arm as she leant forward, listening with a smile upon her parted lips and a light in her eyes that was ineffably tender.

Nearer came the sound, and nearer, until presently, now in the moonlight, now in shadow, there strode a tall, martial figure in all the glory of braided tunic and furred dolman, with three chevrons upon his sleeve, and many shining medals upon his breast.

A stalwart, soldierly figure, despite the one empty sleeve, who moved with the long swinging stride that only the cavalryman can possess. Having come beneath a certain latticed window, the Sergeant halted, and the next moment his glittering sabre flashed up to the salute; then, with it upon his shoulder, he wheeled and began to march up and down.

His spurs jingling, his sabre gleaming, his dolman swinging each time he wheeled, while Miss Priscilla, leaning forward, watched him wide-eyed, and with hands clasped tight.

Then, all at once, with a little fluttering sigh she rose.

Thus the Sergeant, as he marched to and fro, was suddenly aware of one who stood in the full radiance of the moon, and with one hand outstretched towards him.

Now, as he paused, disbelieving his very eyes, he saw that in her extended hand she held a great ripe peach.

"Sergeant," she said, speaking almost in a whisper. "Oh, Sergeant . . . won't you . . . take it?"

The heavy sabre thudded down into the grass, and he took a sudden step towards her. But even now he hesitated, until, coming nearer still, he could look down into her eyes.

Then he spoke, and his voice was very hoarse, and uneven . . .

"Miss Priscilla," he said. "Priscilla? Oh, Priscilla!"

And, with the word, he had fallen on his knees at her feet, and his strong, solitary arm was folded close about her.

Chapter
Five

"What is it, my Porges?"

"Well, I'm a bit worried, you know."

"Worried?"

"Yes; 'fraid I shall be an old man before my time, Uncle Porges. Adam says it's worry that ages a man—an' it killed a cat, too!"

"And why do you worry?"

"Oh, it's my Auntie Anthea, o' course! She was crying again last night . . ."

"Crying!"

Bellew had been lying flat upon his back in the fragrant shadow of the hay-rick, but now he sat up very suddenly—so suddenly that Small Porges started.

"Crying," he repeated, "last night. Are you sure?"

"Oh yes. You see, she forgot to come an' tuck me up last night, so I creeped downstairs, very quietly, you know, to see why. An' I found her bending over the table, all sobbing an' crying.

"At first she tried to pretend that she wasn't, but I saw the tears quite plain—her cheeks were all wet, you know; an' when I put my arms round her to comfort her a bit, an' asked her what was the matter, she only kissed me a lot, an' said, 'Nothing, nothing, only a headache.'"

"And why was she crying, do you suppose, my Porges?"

"Oh, money, of course," he said with a sigh.

"What makes you think it was money?"

"'Cause she'd been talking to Adam; I heard him say, 'Good-night,' as I creeped down the stairs."

"Ah?" said Bellew, staring straight before him.

His beloved pipe had slipped from his fingers and, for a wonder, lay neglected.

"It was after she had talked with Adam, was it, my Porges?"

"Yes, that's why I knew it was 'bout money; Adam's always talking 'bout morgyges an' bills an' money. Oh, Uncle Porges, how I do hate money."

"It is sometimes a confounded nuisance," said Bellew, nodding.

"But I do wish we had some—so we could pay all her bills an' morgyges for her. She'd be so happy, you know, an' go about singing like she used to—an' I shouldn't worry myself into an old man before my time, all wrinkled an' gray, you know, an' all would be revelry an' joy, if only she had enough gold an' bank-notes!"

"And she was crying, you say?" demanded Bellew again, his gaze still far away.

"Yes."

"You are quite sure you saw the tears, my Porges?"

"Oh yes; an' there was one on her nose too, a

big one, that shone awful bright—twinkled, you know."

"And she said it was only a headache, did she?"

"Yes, but that meant money—money always makes her head ache, lately. Oh, Uncle Porges, I s'pose people do find fortunes sometimes, don't they?"

"Why yes, to be sure, they do."

"Then I wish I knew where they looked for them," he said, with a very big sigh indeed. "I've hunted an' hunted in all the attics, an' the cupboards, an' under hedges, an' in ditches, an' prayed an' prayed, you know—every night."

"Then of course you'll be answered, my Porges."

"Do you really s'pose I shall be answered? You see, it's such an awful long way for one small prayer to have to go—from here to Heaven. An' there's clouds that get in the way, an' I'm 'fraid my prayers aren't quite big or heavy enough, an' get lost, an' blown away in the wind."

"No, my Porges," said Bellew, drawing his arm about the small, disconsolate figure, "you may depend upon it that your prayers fly straight up into Heaven, and that neither the clouds nor the wind can come between, or blow them away. So just keep on praying, old chap, and when the time is ripe they'll be answered, never fear."

"Answered—do you mean—oh, Uncle Porges—do you mean—the Money Moon?"

The small hand upon Bellew's arm quivered, and his voice trembled with eagerness.

"Why, yes, to be sure—the Money Moon, my Porges; it's bound to come one of these fine nights."

"Ah, but when—oh, when will the Money Moon ever come?"

"Well, I can't be quite sure, but I rather fancy, from the look of things, my Porges, that it will be pretty soon."

"Oh, I do hope so, for her sake, an' my sake. You see, she may go getting herself married to Mr. Cassilis, if something doesn't happen soon, an' I shouldn't like that, you know."

"Neither should I, my Porges. But what makes you think so?"

"Why, he's always bothering, an' asking her to, you see. She always says 'no,' o' course, but one of these fine days I'm 'fraid she'll say 'yes' accidentally, you know."

"Heaven forbid, nephew!"

"Does that mean you hope not?"

"Indeed, yes."

"Then I say, Heaven forbid, too—because I don't think she'd ever be happy in Mr. Cassilis's great big house, an' I shouldn't either."

"Why, of course not."

"You never go about asking people to marry you, do you, Uncle Porges?"

"Well, it could hardly be called a confirmed habit of mine."

"That's one of the things I like about you so —all the time you've been here you haven't asked my Auntie Anthea once, have you?"

"No, my Porges—not yet."

"Oh, but you don't mean that you ever will?"

"Would you be very grieved and angry if I did, someday soon, my Porges?"

"Well, I—I didn't think you were that kind of man," answered Small Porges, sighing and shaking his head regretfully.

"I'm afraid I am, nephew."

"Do you really mean that you want to marry my Auntie Anthea?"

"I do."

"As much as Mr. Cassilis does?"

"A great deal more, I think."

Small Porges sighed again, and shook his head very gravely indeed.

"Uncle Porges, I'm s'prised at you."

"I rather feared you would be, nephew."

"It's all so awful silly, you know—why want to marry her?"

"Because, like a Prince in a fairy-tale, I'm—er—rather anxious to live happily ever after."

"Oh," said Small Porges, turning this over in his mind. "I never thought of that."

"Marriage is a very important question, you see, my Porges, especially in this case, because I can't possibly live happily ever after unless I marry first, now, can I?"

"No, I s'pose not," Small Porges admitted, albeit reluctantly, after he had pondered the matter awhile with wrinkled brow, "but—but why pick out my Auntie Anthea?"

"Just because she happens to be your Auntie Anthea, of course."

Small Porges sighed again.

"Why then, if she's got to be married someday, so she can live happily ever after—well—I s'pose you'd better take her, Uncle Porges."

"Thank you, old chap—I mean to."

"I'd rather you took her than Mr. Cassilis—an', why, there he is!"

"Who?"

"Why, Mr. Cassilis. An' he's stopped, an' he's twisting his moustache."

Mr. Cassilis, who had been crossing the paddock, had indeed stopped, and was twisting his black moustache, as if he were hesitating between two courses.

Finally he pushed open the gate, and, approaching Bellew, saluted him with that supercilious air which Miss Priscilla always declared she found so "trying."

"Ah, Mr. Bellew, what might it be this morning, the pitchfork, the scythe, or the plough?" he enquired.

"Neither, Sir—this morning it is matrimony."

"Eh! I beg your pardon—matrimony!"

"With a large M, Sir," Bellew nodded, "marriage, Sir, wedlock—my nephew and I are discussing it in its aspects, philosophical, sociological, and . . ."

"That is surely rather a peculiar subject to discuss with a child, Mr. Bellew . . ."

"Meaning my nephew, Sir?"

"I mean young George there."

"Precisely—my nephew, Small Porges."

"I refer," said Mr. Cassilis, with slow and crushing emphasis, "to Miss Devine's nephew . . ."

"And mine, Mr. Cassilis—mine—by—er—mutual adoption and inclination."

"And I repeat that your choice of subjects is peculiar, to say the least of it."

"But then, mine is rather a peculiar nephew, Sir. But surely it is not to discuss nephews, mine or anyone else's, that you are here for, and our ears do wait upon you—pray, be seated, Sir."

"Thank you, I prefer to stand."

"Strange," murmured Bellew, shaking his head, "I never stand if I can sit, or sit if I can lie down."

"I should like you to define, exactly, your position here at Dapplemere, Mr. Bellew."

Bellew's sleepy glance missed nothing of the other's challenging attitude, and his ear missed nothing of Mr. Cassilis's authoritative tone; therefore, his smile was most engaging as he answered:

"My position here, Sir, is truly the most—er—enviable in the world.

"Prudence is an admirable cook—particularly as regards Yorkshire pudding; gentle little Miss Priscilla is the most—er—Aunt-like and perfect of Housekeepers.

"And Miss Anthea is our sovereign lady, before whose radiant beauty Small Porges and I, like true Knights and gallant gentles, do constant homage, and on whose behalf Small Porges and I do stand prepared to wage stern battle, by day or by night."

"Indeed," said Mr. Cassilis, and his smile was even more supercilious than usual.

"Yes, Sir," Bellew nodded, "I do confess me a most fortunate and happy wight, who, having wandered here and there upon this planet of ours, which is so vast, and so very small—has, by the most happy chance, found his way here into Arcadia."

"And may I enquire how long you intend to lead this Arcadian existence?"

"I fear I cannot answer that question until the full o' the moon, Sir—at present, I grieve to say—I do not know."

Mr. Cassilis struck his riding-boot a sudden smart rap with his whip, and his eyes snapped and his nostrils dilated as he glanced down into Bellew's imperturbable face.

"At least you know, and will perhaps explain,

what prompted you to buy all that furniture. You were the only buyer at the sale, I understand."

"Who bought anything, yes," said Bellew, nodding.

"And pray, what was your object—you—a stranger?"

"Well," replied Bellew, slowly, as he began to fill his pipe, "I bought it because it was there to buy, you know; I bought it because furniture is apt to be rather useful, now and then—I acquired the chairs to—er—sit in, the tables to—er—put things on—and . . ."

"Don't quibble with me, Mr. Bellew."

"I beg your pardon, Mr. Cassilis."

"When I ask a question, Sir, I am in the habit of receiving a direct reply."

"And when I am asked a question, Mr. Cassilis, I am in the habit of answering it precisely as I please—or not at all."

"Mr. Bellew, let me impress upon you, once and for all, that Miss Devine has friends—old and tried friends—to whom she can always turn for aid in any financial difficulty she may encounter.

"Friends who can more than tide over all her troubles, without the interference of strangers; and, as one of her oldest friends, I demand to know by what right you force your wholly unnecessary assistance upon her!"

"My very good Sir," returned Bellew, shaking his head in gentle reproof, "really, you seem to forget that you are not addressing one of your grooms, or footmen—consequently, you force me to remind you of the fact; furthermore . . ."

"That is no answer," replied Mr. Cassilis, his gloved hands clenched tight upon his hunting-crop—his whole attitude one of menace.

"Furthermore," pursued Bellew, placidly, settling the tobacco in his pipe with his thumb, "you can continue to—er—demand, until all's blue, and I shall continue to lie here, and smoke, and gaze up at the smiling serenity of Heaven."

The black brows of Mr. Cassilis met in a sudden frown, and he tossed his whip aside and took a sudden quick stride towards the recumbent Bellew, with so evident intention that Small Porges instinctively shrank farther within his encircling arm.

But at that psychic moment, very fortunately for all concerned, there came the sound of a quick, light step, and Anthea stood between them.

"Mr. Cassilis! Mr. Bellew!" she exclaimed, her cheeks flushed, and her bosom heaving with the haste she had made. "Pray, what does this mean?"

Bellew rose to his feet and, seeing that Cassilis was silent, shook his head and smiled.

"Upon my word, I hardly know, Miss Anthea. Our friend Mr. Cassilis seems to have got himself all worked up over the—er—sale, I fancy . . ."

"The furniture!" exclaimed Anthea, and stamped her foot with vexation. "That wretched furniture! Of course you explained your object in buying it, Mr. Bellew?"

"Well, no—we hadn't got as far as that."

Now when he said this, Anthea's eyes flashed sudden scorn at him, and she curled her lip at him and turned her back upon him.

"Mr. Bellew bought my furniture because he intends to set up housekeeping—he is to be married soon, I believe."

"When the moon is at the full," said Bellew, nodding.

"Married!" exclaimed Mr. Cassilis, his frown vanishing as if by magic. "Oh, indeed . . ."

"I am on my way to the hop-gardens, if you care to walk with me, Mr. Cassilis."

With the words, Anthea turned; and as he watched them walk away side by side, Bellew noticed upon the face of Mr. Cassilis an expression very like triumph, and in his general air a suggestion of proprietorship that jarred upon him most unpleasantly.

"Why do you frown so, Uncle Porges?"

"I—er—was thinking, nephew."

"Well, I'm thinking too," said Small Porges, nodding, his brows knitted portentously.

And thus they sat, Big Porges and Little Porges, frowning in unison at space for quite a while.

"Are you quite sure you never told my Auntie Anthea that you were going to marry her?" enquired Small Porges at last.

"Quite sure, comrade—why?"

"Then how did she know you were going to marry her an' settle down?"

"Marry her and settle down?"

"Yes, at the full o' the moon, you know."

"Why, really—I don't know, my Porges—unless she guessed it."

"I specks she did—she's awful clever at guessing things! But do you know . . ."

"Well?"

"I just don't like the way she smiled at Mr. Cassilis; I never saw her look at him like that before—as if she were awful glad to see him, you know; so I don't think I'd wait till the full o' the moon if I were you, I think I'd better marry her this afternoon."

"That," said Bellew, clapping him on the shoulder, "is a very admirable idea—I'll mention it to her on the first available opportunity, my Porges."

But the opportunity did not come that day, nor the next, nor the next after that, for it seemed that with the approach of the "hop-picking," Anthea had no thought or time for anything else.

Wherefore Bellew smoked many pipes, and, as the days wore on, possessed his soul in patience, which is a most excellent precept to follow—in all things but love.

* * *

The house was very quiet, for Small Porges was deep in the vexatious rules of the multiplication-table, and something he called "jogafrey."

Anthea was out, as usual, and Miss Priscilla was busy with her numerous household duties. Thus, the brooding silence was unbroken, save for the occasional murmur of a voice, the jingle of the housekeeping keys, and the quick, light tap-tap of Miss Priscilla's stick.

Therefore, Bellew decided to read the paper, and let it be understood that he regarded the daily news-sheet as the last resource of the utterly bored.

Now presently, as he glanced over the paper with a negative interest, his eye was attracted by a long paragraph that began:

> At St. George's, Hanover Square, by the Right Reverend the Bishop of ——, Silvia Cecilia Marchmont, to His Grace the Duke of Ryde, K.G., K.C.B.

Below followed a full, true, and particular account of the ceremony, which it seemed had been graced by Royalty. George Bellew read it halfway through, and yawned—positively and actually yawned, and thereafter laughed.

"And so I have been in Arcadia—only three weeks! I have known Anthea only twenty-one days! A ridiculously short time, as time goes—in any other place but Arcadia—and yet sufficient to lay forever the—er—Haunting Spectre of the Might Have Been.

"Lord! What a fool I was! Baxter was quite right—utterly and completely right! Now, let us suppose that this paragraph had read:

" 'Today at St. George's, Hanover Square, Anthea Devine to—' No, no—confound it!"

Bellew crumpled up the paper and tossed it into a distant corner.

"I wonder what Baxter would think of me now—good old faithful John. The Haunting Spectre of the Might Have Been—what a preposterous ass—what a monumental idiot I was!"

" 'Posterous ass' isn't a very pretty thing to say, Uncle Porges—or 'continental idiot'!" said a voice behind him, and turning, he saw Small Porges, somewhat stained and bespattered with ink, who shook a reproving head at him.

"True, nephew," he answered, "but they are sometimes very apt, and in this instance particularly so."

Small Porges drew near, and, seating himself upon the arm of Bellew's chair, looked at his adopted Uncle long and steadfastly.

"Uncle Porges," he said at last, "you never tell stories, do you? I mean—lies, you know."

"Indeed, I hope not, Porges—why do you ask?"

"Well, 'cause my Auntie Anthea's 'fraid you do."

"Is she—why?"

"When she came to tuck me up last night, she sat down on my bed an' talked to me a long time, an' she sighed a lot, an' said she was 'fraid I didn't care for her any more—which was awful silly, you know."

"Yes, of course," said Bellew, nodding.

"An' then she asked me why I was fond of you, an' I said 'cause you were my Uncle Porges that I found under a hedge. An' then she got more angrier than ever, an' said she wished I'd left you under the hedge . . ."

"Did she, my Porges?"

"Yes, she said she wished she'd never seen you, an' she'd be awful glad when you'd gone away. So I told her you weren't ever going away, an' that we were waiting for the Money Moon to come an' bring us a fortune.

"An' then she shook her head, an' said, 'Oh, my dear . . . you mustn't believe anything he says to you about the moon, or anything else, 'cause he tells lies,' an' she said 'lies' twice."

"Ah—and—did she stamp her foot, Porges?"

"Yes, I think she did; an' then she said there wasn't such a thing as a Money Moon, and she told me you were going away very soon, to get married, you know."

"And what did you say?"

"Oh, I told her that I was going too. An' then I thought she was going to cry, an' she said, 'Oh, Georgy! I didn't think you'd leave me . . . even for him.'

"So then I had to 'splain how we had arranged that she was going to marry you so that we could all live happily ever after—I mean, that it was all settled, you know, an' that you were going to speak to her on the first opportunity. An' then she looked at me a long time an' asked me was I sure you had said so.

"An' then she got awful angry indeed, an' said, 'How dare he! Oh, how dare he!' So o' course I told her you'd dare anything—even a dragon—'cause you're so big, an' brave, you know.

"So then she went an' stood at the window, an' she was so angry she cried, an' I nearly cried too. But at last she kissed me 'good-night' an' said you were a man that never meant anything you said, an' that I must never believe you any more, an' that you were going away to marry a lady in London an' that she was very glad, 'cause then we should all be happy again, she s'posed.

"So she kissed me again, an' tucked me up an' went away.

"But it was a long, long time before I could go to sleep, 'cause I kept on thinking, an' thinking an' thinking, s'posing there really wasn't any Money Moon after all; s'posing you were going to marry another lady in London! You see, it would all be so frightful awful, wouldn't it?"

"Terribly, awfully dreadful, my Porges."

"But you never do tell lies, do you?"

"No."

"An' there is a Money Moon, isn't there?"

"Why, of course there is."

"An' you are going to marry Auntie Anthea in the full o' the moon, aren't you?"

"Yes, my Porges."

"Why, then—everything's all right again—so let's go an' sit under the hay-stack, an' talk 'bout ships."

"But why of ships?" enquired Bellew, rising.

" 'Cause I made up my mind, this morning, I'd be a sailor when I grow up—a mariner, you know, like Peterday, only I'd prefer to have both my legs."

"You'd find it more convenient, perhaps."

"You know all 'bout oceans, an' waves, and billows, don't you, Uncle Porges?"

"Well, I know a little."

"An' are you ever sea-sick—like a 'land-lubber'?"

"I used to be, but I got over it."

"Was it a very big ship that you came over in?"

"No, not so very big, but she's about as fast as anything in her class, and a cocking sea-boat."

"What's her name?"

"Her name?" repeated Bellew. "Well, she was called the—er—*Silvia*."

"That's an awful pretty name for a ship."

"Hm! So-so—but I have learned a prettier one, and next time she puts out to sea we'll change her name, eh, my Porges?"

"We?" cried Small Porges, looking up with eager eyes. "Do you mean you'd take me to sea with you—an' Auntie Anthea, of course?"

"You don't suppose I'd leave either of you behind if I could help it, do you? We'd all sail away together—wherever you wished."

"You don't mean," said Small Porges, in a suddenly awed voice, "that it is your ship—your very own?"

"Oh yes."

"But—do you know, Uncle Porges, you don't look as though you had a ship—for your very own —somehow."

"Don't I?"

"You see, a ship is such a big thing for one man to have for his very own self. An' has it got masts, an' funnels, an' anchors?"

"Lots of 'em."

"Then, please, when will you take me an' Auntie Anthea sailing all over the oceans?"

"Just as soon as she is ready to come."

"Then I think I'd like to go to Nova Zembla first—I found it in my jogafrey today, an' it sounds nice an' far off, doesn't it?"

"It does, shipmate!" Bellew nodded.

"Oh, that's fine," exclaimed Small Porges, rapturously. "You shall be the Captain, an' I'll be the shipmate, an' we'll say 'Ay, Ay' to each other —like the real sailors do in books—shall we?"

"Ay, ay, shipmate," said Bellew, and nodded again.

"Then, please, Uncle Por—I mean, Captain —what shall we name our ship—I mean the new name?"

"Well, my Porges—I mean, of course, ship-mate—I rather thought of calling her—hallo!— why, there's the Sergeant."

Sure enough, there was Sergeant Appleby sitting under the shade of "King Arthur"—but he rose and stood at attention as they came up.

"Why, Sergeant, how are you?" asked Bellew, gripping the veteran's hand. "You are half-an-hour before your usual time today—nothing wrong, I hope?"

"Nothing wrong, Mr. Bellew, Sir—I thank

you. No, nothing wrong—but this is a memorable occasion, Sir. May I trouble you to—step behind the tree with me—for half a moment, Sir?"

Suiting the action to the word, the Sergeant led Bellew to the other side of the tree, and there, screened from view of the house, he, with a sudden jerky movement, produced a very small leather case from his pocket, which he handed to Bellew.

"Not good enough for such a woman—I know, but the best I could afford, Sir," said the Sergeant, appearing profoundly interested in the leaves overhead, while Bellew opened the very small box.

"Why—it's very handsome, Sergeant," said Bellew, making the jewels sparkle in the sun; "anyone might be proud of such a ring."

"Why, it did look pretty tidy in the shop, Sir —to me, and Peterday. My comrade has a sharp eye, and a sound judgement in most things, and we took a deal of trouble in selecting it. But now when it comes to giving it to her—why, it looks uncommon small, and mean."

"A ruby and two diamonds, and very fine stones, too, Sergeant."

"So I made so bold as to come here," pursued the Sergeant, still interested in the foliage above, "half-an-hour afore my usual time—to ask you, Sir, if you would so far oblige me as to— hand it to her—when I'm gone."

"Lord, no!" said Bellew, smiling and shaking his head. "Not on your life, Sergeant! Why, man, it would lose half its value in her eyes if any other than you gave it to her. No, Sergeant, you must hand it to her yourself, and, what's more, you must slip it upon her finger."

"E'cod, Sir!" exclaimed the Sergeant. "I could never do that!"

"Oh yes you could."

"Not unless you stood by me—a force in reserve, as it were."

"I'll do that willingly, Sergeant."

"Then—p'raps you might happen to know—which finger?"

"The third finger of the left hand, I believe, Sergeant."

"Here's Aunt Priscilla now," said Small Porges, at this juncture.

"Lord!" exclaimed the Sergeant. "And sixteen minutes afore her usual time."

Yes, there was Miss Priscilla, her basket of sewing upon her arm, as gentle and unruffled and placid as usual. And yet it is probable that she divined something from their very attitudes, for there was a light in her eyes, and her cheeks seemed more delicately pink than was their wont.

Then, as she came towards them, under the ancient apple tree, despite her stick and her white hair, she looked even younger and more girlish than ever.

At least, the Sergeant seemed to think so, for as he met her look his face grew suddenly radiant, while a slow flush crept up under the tan of his cheeks, and the solitary hand he held out to her trembled a little, for all its size and strength.

"Miss Priscilla, Mam . . ." he said, and stopped. "Miss Priscilla," he began again, then paused once more.

"Why . . . Sergeant!" she exclaimed, though it was a very soft little exclamation indeed, for her hand still rested in his, and so she could feel the quiver of the strong fingers. "Why . . . Sergeant!"

"Miss Priscilla," he said, beginning all over again, but with no better success.

"Goodness me!" exclaimed Miss Priscilla. "I do believe he is going to forget to enquire about the peaches."

"Peaches!" repeated the Sergeant. "Yes, Priscilla."

"And why?"

"'Cause he's brought you a ring," Small Porges broke in, "a very handsome ring, you know, Aunt Priscilla—all diamonds an' jewels, an' he wants you to please let him put it on your finger —if you don't mind."

"And here it is," said the Sergeant, and gave it into her hand.

Miss Priscilla stood very silent and very still, looking down at the glittering gems; then, all at once, her eyes filled and a slow wave of colour dyed her cheeks.

"Oh, Sergeant," she said very softly. "Oh, Sergeant, I am only a poor old woman . . . with a lame foot."

"And I am a poor old soldier—with only one arm, Priscilla."

"You are the strongest and gentlest and bravest soldier in all the world, I think," she answered.

"And you, Priscilla, are the sweetest and most beautiful woman in the world, I know! And I've loved you all these years, and never dared to tell you so, because of my one arm."

"Why then," said Miss Priscilla, smiling up at him through her tears, "if you do . . . really . . . think that . . . why . . . it's this finger, Sergeant."

So the Sergeant, very clumsily, because he

had but the one hand, slipped the ring upon the finger in question.

And the Porges, Big and Small, turning to glance back, as they went upon their way, saw that he still held that small white hand pressed close to his lips.

"I s'pose they'll be marrying each other one of these fine days!" said Small Porges, as they crossed the meadow side by side.

"Yes, I expect so, shipmate," said Bellew; "and may they live long and die happy, say I."

"Ay, ay, Captain—an' Amen!" returned Small Porges.

So the afternoon wore away to evening, and with evening came Anthea; but a very grave-eyed, troubled Anthea, who sat at the tea-table, silent and preoccupied, so much that small Porges openly wondered, while Miss Priscilla watched over her, wistful and tender.

Thus, tea, which was wont to be the merriest meal of the day, was but the pale ghost of what it should have been, despite Small Porges' flow of conversation (when not impeded by bread and jam) and Bellew's tactful efforts.

Now, while he talked lightheartedly, keeping carefully to generalities, he noticed two things: one was that Anthea made but a pretence of eating; the second, that although she uttered a word now and then, her eyes persistently avoided his.

Thus, he, for one, was relieved when tea was over, and as he rose from the table, he determined, despite the unpropitious look of things, to end the suspense, one way or another, and speak to Anthea just as soon as she should be alone.

But here again he was baulked, and disappointed, for when Small Porges came to bid him "good-night," as usual, he learnt that "Auntie Anthea" had already gone to bed.

"She says it's a headache," said Small Porges, "but I 'speck it's the hops really, you know."

"The hops, my Porges?"

"She's worrying about them; she's 'fraid of a storm, like Adam is. An' when she worries, I worry. Oh, Uncle Porges, if only my prayers can bring the Money Moon soon, you know—very soon.

"If they don't bring it in a day or two, 'fraid I shall wake up one fine morning an' find I've worried an' worried myself into an old man."

"Never fear, shipmate," said Bellew, in his most nautical manner, "all's well that ends well —a-low and aloft all's ataunto.

"So just take a turn at the lee braces, and keep your weather-eye lifted, for you may be sure of this—if the storm does come, it will bring the Money Moon with it."

Then, having bidden Small Porges a cheery "good-night," Bellew went out to walk amongst the roses.

As he walked, he watched the flying rack of clouds above his head and listened to the wind, which moaned in fitful gusts; wherefore, having learnt in his many travels to read and interpret such natural signs and omens, he shook his head and muttered to himself, even as Adam had done before him.

Presently he wandered back into the house, filled his pipe, and went to hold communion with his friend the Cavalier. This was a picture in the Great Hall, which he often sat in front of and talked to.

And thus it was that having ensconced himself in the great elbow-chair and raised his eyes to the picture, he saw a letter tucked into the frame.

Looking closer, he saw that it was directed to himself. He took it down, and after a momentary hesitation broke the seal and read:

> *Miss Devine presents her compliments to Mr. Bellew, and regrets that, owing to unforeseen circumstances, she has to beg that he will provide himself with other quarters at the expiration of the month, being the twenty-third inst.*

Bellew read the lines slowly, twice over, then folded the note very carefully, put it into his pocket, and stood for a long time staring at nothing in particular.

At length he lifted his head and looked up into the smiling eyes of the Cavalier above the mantel.

"Sir," he said very gravely, "it would almost seem that you were in the right of it, that yours is the best method after all."

Then he knocked the ashes from his pipe and went slowly and heavily up to bed.

It was a long time before he fell asleep, but he did so at last, for Insomnia is a demon who rarely finds his way into Arcadia.

But all at once he was awake again, broad awake, and staring into the dark, for a thousand voices seemed to be screaming in his ears, and eager hands were shaking and plucking at window and lattice.

He started up, and then he knew that the

storm was upon them at last, in all its fury, rain
and a mighty wind—a howling, raging tem-
pest.

Yes, a great and mighty wind was abroad; it
shrieked under the eaves, boomed and bellowed
in the chimneys, and roared away to carry de-
struction amongst the distant woods, while the
rain beat and hissed against the window-panes.

Surely in all its many years the old house of
Dapplemere had seldom borne the brunt of such
a storm, so wild, so fierce, and so pitiless!

And, lying there upon his bed, listening to
the uproar and tumult, Bellew must needs think
of her who had once said:

"We are placing all our hopes this year upon
the hops!"

* * *

"Ruined, Sir! Done for! Lord love me, they
ain't worth the trouble of gathering—wot's left
on 'em, Mr. Belloo, Sir."

"So bad as that, Adam?"

"Bad, ah, so bad as ever was, Sir!" said Adam,
blinking suspiciously, and suddenly turning
away.

"Has Miss Anthea seen—does she know?"

"Ah, she were out at dawn, and oh, Lord, Mr.
Belloo, Sir, I can't never forget her poor, stricken
face, so pale and sad it were. But she never
said nothing, but, 'Oh, Adam, my poor hops!'

"An' I see her lips all of a-quiver while she
spoke. An' so she turned away an' came back to
the 'ouse, Sir.

"Poor lass! Oh, poor lass!" he exclaimed, his
voice growing more husky. "She's made a brave
fight for it, but it weren't no use, ye see—it'll be

'good-bye' for her to Dapplemere, after all; that there mortgage can't never be paid now, nohow."

"When is it due?"

"Well, according to the bond, or the deed, or whatever they calls it—it be due—tonight, at nine o'clock, Sir, though old Grimes, as a special favour, an' arter much persuading, agreed to hold over till next Saturday, on account o' the 'op-picking."

"But now—seeing as there ain't no 'ops to be picked—he'll foreclose tonight, an' glad enough to do it, you can lay your oath on that, Mr. Belloo, Sir."

"Tonight," said Bellew, "tonight!" And he stood for a while with bent head, as though lost in profound thought.

"Adam," he said, "help me to harness the mare. I must drive over to the nearest railroad depot—hurry, I must be off, the sooner the better."

"What—be you goin', Sir?"

"Yes; hurry, man—hurry!"

"D' ye mean as you're a-goin' to leave her—now, in the middle of all this trouble?"

"Yes, Adam—I must go to London—on business—now hurry, like a good fellow."

Together they entered the stable and together they harnessed the mare. Which done, not staying for breakfast, Bellew mounted the driver's seat and, with Adam beside him, drove rapidly away.

But Small Porges had seen these preparations, and now came running, all eagerness, but before he could reach the yard, Bellew was out of ear-shot.

So there stood Small Porges, a desolate little

figure, watching the rapid course of the dog-cart until it had vanished over the brow of the hill.

And then all at once the tears welled up into his eyes, hot and scalding, and a great sob burst from him, for it seemed to him that his beloved Uncle Porges had failed him at the crucial moment—had left him solitary just when he needed him most.

Thus, Small Porges gave way to his grief, hidden in the very darkest corner of the stable (where he had retired in case any should observe his weakness), until, having once more gained command of himself, and wiped away his tears with his small and dingy pocket-handkerchief, he slowly recrossed the yard, entered the house, and went to look for his Auntie Anthea.

After much searching he found her, half-lying, half-kneeling, beside his bed. When he spoke to her, though she answered him she did not look up, and he knew that she was weeping.

"Don't, Auntie Anthea, don't," he pleaded. "I know Uncle Porges has gone away an' left us, but you've got me left, you know—an' I shall be a man very soon—before my time, I think, so don't cry—though I'm awful sorry he's gone, too—just when we needed him most, you know?"

"Oh, Georgy!" she whispered. "My dear, brave little Georgy! We shall only have each other soon; they're going to take Dapplemere away from us, and everything we have in the world. Oh, Georgy!"

"Well, never mind!" he said, kneeling beside her, and placing one small arm protectively about her. "We shall always have each other left, you know—nobody shall ever take you away from me.

"An' then there's the Money Moon! It's been

an awful long time coming, but it may come to-night, or tomorrow night, he said it would be sure to come if the storm came, an' so I'll find the fortune for you at last.

"I know I shall find it someday, o' course—'cause I've prayed an' prayed for it so very hard, an' he said my prayers went straight up to Heaven, an' didn't get blown away or lost in the clouds.

"So don't cry, Auntie Anthea; let's wait—just a little longer, till the Money Moon comes."

Chapter
Six

"Baxter."

"Sir?"

"Get me a pen and ink."

"Yes, Sir."

Now, any ordinary mortal might have manifested just a little surprise to see his master suddenly walk in, dusty and dishevelled of person, his habitual languor entirely laid aside, and to thus demand pen and ink forthwith.

But then, Baxter, though mortal, was the very cream of gentlemen's gentlemen, and the acme of valets (as has been said), and he comported himself accordingly.

"Baxter."

"Sir?"

"Oblige me by getting this cashed."

"Yes, Sir."

"Bring half of it in gold."

"Yes, Sir. Sir," said Baxter, glancing down at the slip of paper, "did you say—half, Sir?"

"Yes, Baxter—I'd take it all in gold, only that it would be rather awkward to drag around. So bring half in gold and the rest in five-pound notes."

"Very good, Sir."

"And—Baxter."

"Sir?"

"Take a cab."

"Certainly, Sir."

Baxter went out, closing the door behind him. Meanwhile, Bellew busied himself in removing all traces of his journey, and was already bathed and shaved and dressed by the time Baxter returned.

Now, gripped in his right hand, Baxter carried a black leather bag, which jingled as he set it down upon the table.

"Got it?" enquired Bellew.

"I have, Sir."

"Good," said Bellew. "Now, just run around to the garage and fetch the new racing-car—the Mercedes."

"Now, Sir?"

"Now, Baxter."

Once more Baxter departed, and while he was gone, Bellew began to pack—that is to say, he bundled coats and trousers and shirts and boots into a portmanteau in a way that would have wrung Baxter's heart, could he have seen.

When this was done, Bellew opened the black bag, glanced inside, shut it again, and, lighting his pipe, stretched himself out upon an ottoman, and immediately became immersed in thought.

So lost was he, indeed, that Baxter, upon his return, was forced to emit three distinct coughs (the most perfectly proper and gentleman-like coughs in the world) before Bellew was aware of his presence.

"Oh, that you, Baxter?" he said, sitting up. "Back so soon?"

"The car is at the door, Sir."

"The car—ah, yes, to be sure—Baxter."

"Sir?"

"What should you say if I told you . . ."

Bellew paused to strike a match, broke it, tried another, broke that, and finally put his pipe back into his pocket, very conscious all the while of Baxter's steady though perfectly respectful regard.

"Baxter," he said again.

"Sir?"

"What should you say if I told you that I was in love—at last, Baxter! Head over ears—hopelessly —irretrievably?"

"Say, Sir? Why, I should say, 'Indeed, Sir?' "

"What should you say," pursued Bellew, staring thoughtfully down at the rug under his feet, "if I told you that I am so very much in love that I am positively afraid to tell her so?"

"I should say, 'Very remarkable, Sir!' "

Bellew took out his pipe again, looked at it very much as if he had never seen such a thing before, and laid it down upon the mantelpiece.

"Baxter," he went on, "kindly understand that I am speaking to you as—er—man to man— as my Father's old and trusted servant and my early boyhood's only friend; sit down, John."

"Thank you, Master George, Sir."

"I wish to confess to you, John, that—er— regarding the—er—Haunting Spectre of the Might Have Been, you were entirely in the right. At that time I knew no more the meaning of the—er—the word, John . . ."

"Meaning the word 'love,' Master George?"

"Precisely; I knew no more about it than—that table. But during these latter days I have begun to understand, and—er—the fact of the matter is, I'm—I'm fairly up against it, John."

Here, Baxter, who had been watching him with his quick, sharp eyes, nodded his head solemnly.

"Master George," he answered, "speaking as your Father's old servant, and your boyhood's friend—I'm afraid you are."

Bellew took a turn up and down the room, and then, pausing in front of Baxter (who had risen also, as a matter of course), he suddenly laid his two hands upon his valet's shoulders.

"Baxter," he said, "you'll remember that after my Mother died, my Father was always too busy piling up his millions to give much time or thought to me, and I should have been a very lonely boy if it hadn't been for you, John Baxter.

"I was often 'up against it' in those days, John, and you were always ready to help and advise me; but now—well, from the look of things, I'm rather afraid that I must stay 'up against it'—that the game is lost already, John.

"But whichever way Fate decides—win or lose —I'm glad, yes, very glad to have learned the true meaning of the word, John."

"Master George, Sir, there was a poet once —Tennyson, I think—who said, ' 'Tis better to have loved and lost than never to have loved at all,' and I know that he was right.

"Many years ago, before you were born, Master George, I loved, and lost, and that is how I know. But I hope that Fortune will be kinder to you, indeed I do."

"Thank you, John, though I don't see why she should be."

Bellew stood staring down at the rug again, till aroused by Baxter's cough.

"Pray, Sir, what are your orders? The car is waiting downstairs."

"Orders? Why—er—pack your grip, Baxter. I shall take you with me, this time into Arcadia, Baxter."

"For how long, Sir?"

"Probably a week."

"Very good, Sir."

"It is now half-past three; I must be back in Dapplemere at eight. Take your time; I'll go down to look at the machine. Just lock the place up, and—er—don't forget the black bag."

As they drove they talked, not as master and servant but as "between man and man."

"So you see, John, if all things do go well with me, we should probably take a trip to the Mediterranean."

"In the *Silvia*, of course, Master George?"

"Yes; though—er—I've decided to change her name, John."

"Ah! Very natural—under the circumstances, Master George," said honest John, his eyes twinkling slyly as he spoke. "Now, if I might suggest a new name, it would be hard to find a more original one than *The Haunting Spectre of the . . .*"

"Bosh, John, there never was such a thing. You were quite right, as I said before, and—by Heaven—potato-sacks!"

"Eh, what? Potato-sacks, Master George?"

They had been climbing a long, winding ascent, but now, having reached the top of the hill, they overtook a great, lumbering market-cart, or wain, piled high with sacks of potatoes, and driven by an extremely surly-faced man in a smock-frock.

"Hallo there!" cried Bellew, slowing up. "How much for one of your potato-sacks?"

"Get out, now!" growled the surly-faced man, in a tone as surly as his look. "Can't ye see as they're all occipied?"

"Well—empty one."

"Get out, now!" repeated the man, his scowl blacker than ever.

"I'll give you a sovereign for one."

"Now, don't ye try none o' your jokes wi' me, young feller!" growled the carrier. "Sovereign, bah—show me!"

"Here it is!" said Bellew, holding up the coin in question. "Catch!"

With the word, he tossed it up to the carter, who caught it, very dexterously, looked at it, bit it, rubbed it on his sleeve, rang it upon the footboard of his wagon, bit it again, and finally—pocketed it.

"It's a go," he said with a nod, his scowl vanishing as if by magic, and as he spoke, he turned, seized the nearest sack, and forthwith sent a cascade of potatoes rolling and bounding all over the road.

Then he folded up the sack and handed it down to Bellew, who thrust it under the seat, nodded, threw in the clutch, and set off down the road.

But, long after the car had hummed itself out of sight, and the dust of its going had subsided, the carter sat staring after it—open-mouthed.

If Baxter wondered at this purchase, he said nothing; he only bent his gaze thoughtfully upon the black leather bag that he held upon his knee.

On they sped, between fragrant hedges, under whispering trees, past lonely cottage and farm-house, past gate and field and wood, until the sun grew low.

At last Bellew stopped the automobile at a place where a narrow lane, or cart-track, branched off from the high-road and wound away between great trees.

"I leave you here," he said as he sprang from the car. "This is Dapplemere; the farm-house lies over the upland, yonder—though you can't see it because of the trees."

"Is it far, Master George?"

"About a half-mile."

"Here is the bag, Sir, but do you think it is— quite safe?"

"Safe, John?"

"Under the circumstances, Master George, I think it would be advisable to—to take this with you."

He held out a small revolver, and Bellew laughed and shook his head.

"Such things aren't necessary here in Arcadia, John; besides, I have my stick. So, good-bye for the present; you'll stay at the King's Head, remember."

"Good-night, Master George, Sir, good-night, and good fortune go with you."

"Thank you," said Bellew, and reached out his hand. "I think we'll shake on that, John."

So they clasped hands, and Bellew turned and set off along the grassy lane, and presently, as he went, he heard the hum of the car rapidly growing fainter and fainter until it was lost in the quiet of the evening.

The shadows were creeping down and evening was approaching as Bellew took his way along that winding lane that led to the house of Dapplemere.

Had there been anyone to see (which there was not), they might have noticed something almost furtive in his manner of approach, for he walked always under the trees where the shadows lay thickest, and paused once or twice to look about him warily.

Coming within sight of the house, he turned aside, and, forcing his way through a gap in the hedge, came by a round-about course to the farmyard.

Here, after some searching, he discovered a spade, which (having discarded his stick) he took upon his shoulder, and with the black leather bag tucked under his arm, he crossed the paddock with the same degree of caution, and so at last reached the orchard.

On he went, always in the shadow, till he paused beneath the mighty, knotted branches of "King Arthur."

He quickly put the money in the potato-sack and dug a hole to bury it under "King Arthur."

Evening had deepened into night—a night of ineffable calm, a night of all-pervading quietude. A horse snorted in the stable near-by, and a dog barked in the distance, but these sounds served only to render the silence more profound by contrast.

It was indeed a night wherein pixies and elves, and goblins and fairies, might weave their magic spells; a night wherein tired humanity dreamt those dreams that seem so hopelessly impossible by day.

And over all the moon rose higher and higher, in solemn majesty, filling the world with her pale loveliness, and brooding over it like the gentle goddess she is.

Even the dog in the distance seemed to feel something of all this, for after a futile bark or two he gave it up altogether, and was heard no more.

And Bellew, gazing up at Luna's pale serenity, smiled and nodded—as much as to say, "You'll do," and stood leaning upon his spade, listening to:

> *That deep hush which seems a sigh*
> *Breathed by earth to listening sky.*

Now, all at once, upon this quietude there came a voice upraised in fervent supplication. Treading very softly, Bellew came, and, peeping round the hay-rick, saw Small Porges upon his knees.

He was equipped for travelling and the perils of the road, for beside him lay a stick, and tied to this stick was a bundle that bulged with his most cherished possessions.

His cheeks were wet with great tears that glistened in the moon-beams, but he wept with eyes shut tight, and with his small hands clasped close together; and thus he spoke, albeit much shaken and hindered by sobs.

"I s'pose you think I bother you an awful lot, dear Lord—an' so do I, but you haven't sent the Money Moon yet, you see, an' now my Auntie Anthea's got to leave Dapplemere—if I don't find the fortune for her soon.

"I know I'm crying a lot, an' real men don't cry, but it's only 'cause I'm awful lonely an' disappointed, an' nobody can see me, so it doesn't matter.

"But, dear Lord, I've looked and looked everywhere, an' I haven't found a single sovereign yet, an' I've prayed to you an' prayed to you for the Money Moon, an' it's never come.

"So now, dear Lord, I'm going to Africa, an' I want you to please take care of my Auntie Anthea till I come back.

"Sometimes I'm 'fraid my prayers can't quite manage to get up to you, 'cause of the clouds an' wind, but tonight there isn't any, so if they do reach you, please—oh, please let me find the fortune, and please, if you don't mind, let him come back to me—dear Lord—I mean my Uncle Porges, you know.

"An' now—that's all, dear Lord, so Amen."

As the prayer ended, Bellew stole back, and, coming to the gate of the rick-yard, leant there, waiting. And presently, as he watched, he saw a small figure emerge from behind the big haystack and come striding manfully towards him, his bundle upon his shoulders, and with the moon bright in his curls.

But all at once Small Porges saw him and stopped, and the stick and bundle fell to the ground and lay neglected.

"Why—my Porges!" said Bellew, a trifle huskily perhaps. "Why, shipmate!" And he held out his hands.

Then Small Porges uttered a cry and came

running; the next moment Big Porges had him in his arms.

"Oh, Uncle Porges! Then you have come back to me!"

"Ay, ay, shipmate."

"Why then—my prayers did reach!"

"Of course; prayers always reach, my Porges."

"Then—oh—do you s'pose I shall find the fortune too?"

"Not a doubt of it—just look at the moon!"

"The moon?"

"Why, haven't you noticed how—er—peculiar it is tonight?"

"Peculiar?" repeated Small Porges breathlessly, turning to look at it.

"Why, yes, my Porges—big, you know, and —er—yellow, like—er—like a very large sovereign."

"Do you mean—oh, do you mean—it's— the . . ."

But here Small Porges choked suddenly, and could only look his question.

"The Money Moon? Oh, yes—there she is at last, my Porges; take a good look at her, for I don't suppose we shall ever see another."

Small Porges stood very still and gazed up at the moon's broad yellow disc, and as he looked, the tears welled up in his eyes again and a great sob broke from him.

"I'm so—glad," he whispered. "So—awful glad!"

Then suddenly he dashed away his tears and slipped his small, trembling hand into Bellew's.

"Quick, Uncle Porges," he said. "Mr. Grimes is coming tonight, you know—an' we must find the money in time. Where shall we look for it?"

"Well, I guess the orchard will do—to start with."

"Then let's go—now."

"But we shall need a couple of spades, shipmate."

"Oh, must we dig?"

"Yes—I fancy that's a—er—diggin' moon, my Porges, from the look of it. Ah! There's a spade nice and handy; you take that, and I'll—er—I'll manage with this pitchfork."

"But you can't dig with a . . ."

"Oh! Well, you can do the digging, and I'll just—er—prod, you know. Ready—then heave ahead, shipmate."

So they set out, hand in hand, spade and pitchfork on shoulder, and presently came to the orchard.

"It's an awful' big place to dig up a fortune in!" said Small Porges, glancing about. "Where do you s'pose we'd better begin?"

"Well, shipmate, between you and me and the pitchfork here, I rather fancy 'King Arthur' knows much more than most people would think; anyway, we'll try him. You dig on that side and I'll prod on this."

Saying which, Bellew pointed to a certain spot where the grass looked somewhat uneven and peculiarly bumpy, and, bidding Small Porges get to work, went round to the other side of the great tree.

Being there, he took out his pipe, purely from force of habit, and stood with it clenched in his teeth, listening to the scrape of Small Porges' spade.

Presently he heard a cry, a panting, breathless cry, but one which was full of a joy unspeakable.

"I've got it! Oh, Uncle Porges—I've found it!"

Small Porges was down upon his knees, pulling and tugging at a sack he had partially unearthed, and which, with Bellew's aid, he dragged forth into the moonlight.

In the twinkling of an eye the string was cut, and, plunging in a small hand, Porges brought up a fist full of shining sovereigns, and amongst them a crumpled bank-note.

"It's all right, Uncle Porges!" he exclaimed, nodding, his voice all a-quaver. "It's all right now —I've found the fortune I've prayed for—gold, you know, an' bank-notes—in a sack. Everything will be all right again now."

While he spoke, he rose to his feet, lifted the sack with an effort, swung it across his shoulder, and set off towards the house.

"Is it heavy, shipmate?"

"Awful heavy!" he said, panting. "But I don't mind that—it's gold, you see!"

But, as they crossed the rose-garden, Bellew laid a restraining hand upon his shoulder.

"Porges," he said, "where is your Auntie Anthea?"

"In the drawing-room, waiting for Mr. Grimes."

"Then come this way," said Bellew, and, turning, he led Small Porges up and along the terrace.

"Now, my Porges," he admonished him, "when we come to the drawing-room window— they're open, you see—I want you to hide with me in the shadows, and wait until I give you the word."

"Ay, ay, Captain!" said Small Porges, still panting.

"When I say, 'Heave ahead, shipmate,' why then, you will take your treasure upon your back, and march straight into the room—you understand?"

"Ay, ay, Captain."

"Why then—come on, and mum's the word, shipmate."

Very cautiously they approached the long French windows, and paused in the shadow of a great rose-bush near-by. From where he stood Bellew could see Anthea, and Miss Priscilla, and between them, sprawling in an easy-chair, was Grimes, while Adam, hat in hand, scowled in the background.

"All I can say is as I'm very sorry for ye, Miss Anthea," Grimes was saying. "Ah, that I am, but glad as you've took it so well—no crying or nonsense!"

Here he turned to look at Miss Priscilla, whose everlasting sewing had fallen to her feet and lay there unnoticed, while her tearful eyes were fixed upon Anthea, standing white-faced beside her.

"And when—when shall ye be ready to leave, to—vacate Dapplemere, Miss Anthea?" Grimes went on. "Not as I mean to 'urry you, mind—only I should like you to name a day."

Now as Bellew watched, he saw Anthea's lips move, but no sound came; Miss Priscilla saw also, and, catching the nerveless hand, drew it to her bosom and wept over it.

"Come, come," expostulated Grimes, jingling the money in his pockets. "Come, come, Miss Anthea, Ma'am—all as I'm axing you is, when? All as I want you to do is . . ."

But here Adam, who had been screwing and wringing at his hat, stepped forward, tapped Grimes upon the shoulder, and pointed to the door.

"Mr. Grimes," he said, "Miss Anthea's told ye all as you come here to find out; she's told you as she can't pay, so now s'pose you—go."

"But all I want to know is when she'll be ready to move, and I ain't a-going till I do—so you get out o' my way."

"S'pose you go," repeated Adam.

"Get out o' my way—d' ye hear?"

"Because," Adam went on, "if you don't, Mr. Grimes, the 'Old Adam' be raising inside o' me to that degree as I shall be forced to ketch you by the collar o' your jacket and heave you out, Mr. Grimes—Sir—so s'pose you go."

Hereupon Mr. Grimes rose, put on his hat, and, muttering to himself, stamped indignantly from the room, and Adam, shutting the door upon him, turned to Miss Anthea, who stood white-lipped and dry-eyed, while gentle little Miss Priscilla fondled her listless hand.

"Don't—don't look that way, Miss Anthea," said Adam. "I'd rather see you cry than look so. It be 'ard to 'ave to let the old place go—but . . ."

"Heave ahead, shipmate!" whispered Bellew.

Obedient to his command, Small Porges, with his burden upon his back, ran forward and stumbled into the room.

"It's all right, Auntie Anthea!" he cried. "I've

got the fortune for you—I've found the money I prayed for; here it is, oh—here it is!"

The sack fell, jingling, to the floor, and the next moment he had poured a heap of shining gold and crumpled bank-notes at Anthea's feet.

For a moment no-one moved; then, with a strange, hoarse cry, Adam flung himself down upon his knees and caught up a great handful of the gold, while Miss Priscilla sobbed, with her arms about Small Porges.

Anthea stared down at the treasures, wide-eyed, and with her hands pressed down upon her heart; Adam gave a sudden great laugh, and, springing up, went running out through the window, never spying Bellew in his haste, and shouting as he ran.

"Grimes!" he roared. "Oh, Grimes, come back an' be paid! Come back—we've had our little joke wi' you—now come back an' be paid!"

Then at last Anthea's stony calm was broken, and her bosom heaved with tempestuous sobs; the next moment she had thrown herself upon her knees and had clasped her arms about Small Porges and Aunt Priscilla, mingling her tears with theirs.

As for Bellew, he turned away, and, treading a familiar path, found himself beneath the shadow of "King Arthur."

He sat down, lit his pipe, and stared up at the glory of the full, orbed moon.

"Happiness," he said, speaking his thoughts aloud, "happiness shall come riding astride the full moon. Now—I wonder . . ."

At length, however, he rose and turned his steps towards the house.

"Mr. Bellew!"

He started and turned, and saw Anthea standing amongst her roses.

For a moment they looked at each other in silence, as though each dreaded to speak; then suddenly she turned, and broke a fresh rose from its stem, and stood twisting it between her fingers.

"Why did you . . . do it?" she asked.

"Do it?" he repeated.

"I mean the fortune. Georgy told me . . . how you helped him to find it, and I . . . know how it came to be there. Why did you . . . do it?"

"You didn't tell him—how it came to be there?" Bellew asked anxiously.

"No," she answered. "I think it would have broken his heart . . . if he knew."

"And I think it would have broken his heart if he had never found it," said Bellew, "and I couldn't let that happen, could I?"

Anthea did not answer, and he saw that her eyes were very bright in the shadows of her lashes, though she kept them lowered to the rose in her fingers.

"Anthea," he said suddenly, and reached out his hand to her.

But she started and drew back from his touch.

"Don't," she said, speaking almost in a whisper, "don't touch me. Oh! I know you have paid off the mortgage . . . you have bought back my home for me as you bought back my furniture! Why? Why?

"I was nothing to you, nor you to me. Why have you laid me under this obligation? You know I can never hope to return your money. Oh, why . . . why did you do it?"

"Because I love you, Anthea, have loved you from the first. Because everything I possess in this world is yours—even as I am."

"You forget," she broke in proudly, "you forget . . ."

"Everything but my love for you, Anthea—everything but that I want you for my wife. I'm not much of a fellow, I know, but could you learn to love me enough to—marry me—someday, Anthea?"

"Would you have . . . dared to say this to me . . . before tonight, before the money had bought back the roof over my head? Oh, haven't I been humiliated enough?

"You . . . you have taken from me the only thing I had left . . . my independence . . . stolen it from me. Oh, hadn't I been shamed enough?"

Now as she spoke she saw that his eyes had grown suddenly big and fierce, and in that moment her hands were in his powerful clasp.

"Let me go!" she cried.

"No," he said, shaking his head, "not until you tell me if you love me. Speak, Anthea."

"Loose my hands!"

She threw up her head proudly, and her eyes gleamed, and her cheeks flamed with sudden anger.

"Loose me!" she repeated.

But Bellew only shook his head, and his chin seemed rather more prominent than usual as he answered:

"Tell me that you love me, or that you hate me—whichever it is, but until you do . . ."

"You . . . hurt me," she answered; and then, as his fingers relaxed, with a sudden passionate cry she broke free, but even so, he caught and swept her up in his arms, and held her close against his breast.

And now, feeling the hopelessness of further struggle, she lay passive, while her eyes flamed up into his, and his eyes looked down into hers.

Her long, thick hair had come loose, and now, with a sudden, quick gesture, she drew it across her face, veiling it from him, where he stooped his head above those lustrous tresses.

"Anthea," he murmured, and the masterful voice was strangely hesitating, and the masterful arms about her were wonderfully gentle. "Anthea —do you love me?"

Lower he bent, and lower, until his lips touched her hair, until, beneath that fragrant veil, his mouth sought and found hers, and in that breathless moment he felt them quiver in response to his caress.

And then he set her down and she was free, and he was looking at her with a new-found radiance in his eyes.

"Anthea," he said wonderingly, "why then —you do . . ."

But as he spoke she hid her face in her hands.

"Anthea," he repeated.

"Oh!" she whispered. "I . . . hate you . . . despise you. Oh, you shall be paid back . . . every penny, every farthing, and . . . very soon. Next week . . . I shall marry Mr. Cassilis!"

And so she turned and fled away, and left him standing there amongst the roses.

* * *

Bellew gazed down from the frowning Heaven to the gloom of earth below, with its ever-moving misty shapes, and shivered involuntarily.

In another hour it would be day, and with the day the gates of Arcadia would open for his departure, and he must go forth to become once more a wanderer, going up and down and to and fro in the world until his course had run.

And yet it was worth having lived for, this one golden month; and in all his wanderings he must carry with him the memory of her, who had taught him how deep and high, how wide and infinitely far-reaching, that thing called "love" may really be.

And Porges—dear, quaint, Small Porges— where under Heaven could he ever find again such utter faith, such pure unaffected loyalty and devotion, as throbbed within that small, warm heart?

How could he ever bid good-bye to loving, eager, little Small Porges?

And then there was Miss Priscilla, and the strong gentle Sergeant, and Peterday, and sturdy Adam, and Prudence, and the rosy-cheeked maids.

How well they all suited this wonderful Arcadia! Yes, indeed he and he only had been out-of-place, and so he must go back to the every-day, matter-of-fact world, but how could he ever say good-bye to faithful, loving Small Porges?

Bellew descended the great, wide stair, soft of foot and cautious of step, yet paused once to look towards a certain closed door, and so presently let himself quietly out into the dawn.

The dew sparkled in the grass and hung in glittering jewels from every leaf and twig, while now and then a shining drop would fall upon him as he paused, like a great tear.

Now as he reached the orchard up rose the sun

in all his majesty, filling the world with the splendour of his coming—before whose kindly beams the skulking mists and shadows shrank, afraid, and fled utterly away.

This morning "King Arthur" wore his grandest robes of state, for his mantle of green was thick-sewn with a myriad of flaming gems.

Bellew paused to lay a hand upon its mighty, rugged bole, and while doing so, he turned and looked back at the house of Dapplemere.

And truly never had the old house seemed as beautiful, as quaint, and as peaceful as it did now.

Its every stone and beam had become familiar and, as he looked, seemed to find an individuality of its own; the very lattices seemed to look back at him like so many wistful eyes.

Therefore, George Bellew, American Citizen, millionaire, traveller, explorer, and—*lover*—sighed as he turned away and strode on through the green and golden morning, and resolutely looked back no more.

Bellew walked on at a good pace, with his back turned resolutely towards the house of Dapplemere, and then as he swung into that narrow, grassy lane that wound away between trees, he was much surprised to hear a distant hail.

Facing sharply about, he espied a diminutive figure whose small legs trotted very fast, and whose small fist waved a weather-beaten cap.

Bellew's first impulse was to turn and run, but Bellew rarely acted on impulse; therefore, he set down his bulging portmanteau, seated himself upon it, took out pipe and tobacco, and waited for his pursuer to come up.

"Oh, Uncle Porges, you did walk so awful fast, an' I called an' called you, but you never heard. An' now, please—where are you going?"

"Going," said Bellew, searching through his pockets for a match, "going, my Porges, why—er —for a stroll, to be sure—just a walk before breakfast, you know."

"But then—why have you brought your bag?"

"Bag!" repeated Bellew, stooping down to look at it. "Why—so—I have."

"Please—why?" persisted Small Porges, suddenly anxious. "Why did you bring it?"

"Well, I expect it was to—er—to bear me company, but how is it that you are out so very early, my Porges?"

"Why, I couldn't sleep last night, you know, 'cause I kept on thinking 'bout the fortune, so I got up—in the middle of the night—an' dressed myself, an' sat in the big chair by the window, an' looked at the Money Moon, and stared at it, an' stared at it until a wonderful thing happened —an' what do you s'pose?"

"I don't know."

"Well—all at once, while I stared up at it, the moon changed itself into a great big face, but I didn't mind a bit, 'cause it was a very nice sort of face, rather like a gnome's face, only without the beard, you know.

"An' while I looked at it, it talked to me, an' told me a lot of things—an' that's how I know that you are going away, 'cause you are, you know—aren't you?"

"Why, my Porges," said Bellew, fumbling with his pipe, "why, shipmate, since you ask me, I am."

"Yes, I was 'fraid the moon was right," said Small Porges, and turned away.

But Bellew had seen the stricken look in his eyes, and therefore, he took Small Porges into the circle of his big arm, and, holding him thus, explained to him that in this great world each of us must walk his appointed way, and that there must and always will be partings, but that also there must and always shall be meetings.

"And so, my Porges, if we have to say good-bye now, the sooner we shall meet again—some-day—somewhere."

But Small Porges only sighed, and shook his head in hopeless dejection.

"Does she know you're going, I mean my Auntie Anthea?"

"Oh yes, she knows, Porges."

"Then I s'pose that's why she was crying so, in the night . . ."

"Crying?"

"Yes; she's cried an awful lot lately, hasn't she? Last night when I woke up, you know, an' couldn't sleep, I went into her room, an' she was crying, with her face half-hidden in the pillow, an' her hair all about her . . ."

"Crying!"

"Yes, an' she said she wished she was dead. So o' course I tried to comfort her, you know, an' she said, 'I'm a dreadful failure, Georgy dear, with the farm an' everything else. I've tried to be a father and mother to you, an' I've failed in that too; so now I'm going to give you a real father."

"An' she told me she was going to marry Mr. Cassilis. But I said 'no'—'cause I'd 'ranged for her to marry you an' live happily ever after. But she got awful angry again, an' said she'd never marry you if you were the last man in the world, 'cause she 'spised you so . . ."

"And that would seem to settle it," said Bellew, nodding gloomily, "so it's 'good-bye,' my Porges; we may as well shake hands now and get it over." Bellew rose from the portmanteau and, sighing, held out his hand.

"Oh, but wait a minute," cried Small Porges eagerly, "I haven't told you what the moon said to me last night . . ."

"Ah, to be sure, we were forgetting that!" said Bellew, with an absent look, and a trifle wearily.

"Why then, please sit down again, so I can speak into your ear, 'cause what the moon told me to tell you was a secret, you know."

So Bellew reseated himself upon his portmanteau, and drawing Small Porges close, bent his head down to the anxious little face, and so Small Porges told him exactly what the moon had said.

And the moon's message (whatever it was) seemed to be very short and concise (as all really important messages should be); but those few words had a wondrous and magical effect upon George Bellew.

For a moment he stared wide-eyed at Small Porges like one awakening from a dream, and then the gloom vanished from his brow and he sprang to his feet.

And, being upon his feet, he hit his clenched fist down into the palm of his hand with a resounding smack.

"By Heaven!" he exclaimed, and took a turn across the width of the lane and back again, and, seeing Small Porges watching him, he suddenly caught him up in his arms and hugged him.

"And the moon will be at the full tonight!" he said.

Thereafter he sat down upon his portmanteau again, with Small Porges upon his knee, and they talked confidentially, with their heads very close together, and in muffled tones.

When at last Bellew rose, his eyes were bright and eager, and his square chin was prominent and grimly resolute.

"So—you quite understand, my Porges?"

"Yes, yes—oh, I understand."

"Where the little bridge spans the brook— the trees are thicker there."

"Ay, ay—Captain."

"Then fare thee well, shipmate. Good-bye, my Porges—and remember."

So they clasped hands very solemnly, Big Porges and Small Porges, and each turned his appointed way, the one up and the other down the lane.

But lo, as they went, Small Porges' tears were banished quite, and Bellew strode upon his way, his head held high and his shoulders squared like one in whom hope has been new-born.

Chapter Seven

"And so . . . he has . . . really gone."

Miss Priscilla sighed as she spoke, and looked up from her needlework to watch Anthea, who sat, biting her pen and frowning down at the blank sheet of paper before her.

"And so he is . . . really . . . gone."

"Who . . . Mr. Bellew? Oh, yes."

"He went . . . very early."

"Yes."

"And . . . without any breakfast."

"That was . . . his own fault," Anthea said.

"And without even saying good-bye."

"Perhaps he was in a hurry," Anthea suggested.

"Oh dear me, no, my dear—I don't believe Mr. Bellew was ever in a hurry in all his life."

"No," said Anthea, giving her pen a vicious bite, "I don't believe he ever was; he is always so . . . hatefully placid, and deliberate."

She bit her pen again.

"Eh, my dear?" exclaimed Miss Priscilla, pausing, with her needle in mid-air. "Did you say . . . 'hatefully'?"

"Yes."

"Anthea!"

"I . . . hate him, Aunt Priscilla."

"Eh . . . my dear!"

"That was why I . . . sent him away."

"You sent him away?"

"Yes."

"But, Anthea, why?"

"Oh, Aunt Priscilla . . . surely you never believed in the . . . fortune? Surely you guessed it was . . . his money that paid back the mortgages . . . didn't you, Aunt . . . didn't you?"

"Well, my dear, but then, he did it so very tactfully, and, and, I had hoped, my dear, that . . ."

"That I should . . . marry him and settle the obligation that way, perhaps?"

"Well, yes, my dear, I did hope so . . ."

"Oh, I'm going to marry . . ."

"Then why did you send—"

"I'm going to marry Mr. Cassilis, whenever he pleases."

"Anthea!" The word was a cry, and the needlework slipped from Miss Priscilla's nerveless fingers.

"He asked me to write and tell him if ever I changed my mind."

"Oh, my dear, my dear!" cried Miss Priscilla, reaching out imploring hands. "You never mean it; you are all distraught today, tired, and worn out with worry, and loss of sleep. Wait."

"Wait!" repeated Anthea bitterly. "For what?"

"To marry him! Oh, Anthea, you never mean it! Think . . . think what you are doing."

"I thought of it all last night, Aunt Priscilla, and all this morning, and I have made up my mind."

"You mean to write?"

"Yes."

"To tell Mr. Cassilis that you will . . . marry him?"

"Yes."

But now Miss Priscilla rose, and the next moment she was kneeling beside Anthea's chair.

"Oh, my dear," she pleaded, "you know that I love you like my own flesh and blood . . . don't, oh, Anthea, don't do what can never be undone . . . don't give your youth and beauty to one who can never . . . never make you happy; oh, Anthea . . ."

"Dear Aunt Priscilla, I would rather marry one I don't love than have to live beholden all my days to a man that I . . . hate."

Now as she spoke, though her embrace was as ready and her hands as gentle as ever, yet Miss Priscilla saw that her proud face was set and stern.

So, sighing, she presently rose and, taking her little crutch-stick, dolefully tapped away and left Anthea to write her letter.

Hesitating no more, Anthea took up her pen and wrote, surely a very short missive for a love-letter, and when she had folded and sealed it, she tossed it aside and, laying her arms upon the table, hid her face, with a long, shuddering sigh.

In a little while she rose, took up the letter, and went out to find Adam; but, remembering that he had gone to Cranbrook with Small Porges, she paused, irresolute, and then turned her steps towards the orchard.

But, hearing voices, she stopped again, and, glancing about, saw the Sergeant and Miss Priscilla; she had given both her hands into the Sergeant's one, and he was looking down at her, and she up at him, and upon the face of each was a great and shining joy.

Now, seeing all this, Anthea felt herself very lonely all at once, and, turning aside, she saw all things through the blur of sudden tears.

She was possessed also of a sudden, fierce loathing of the future, a horror because of the promise her letter contained. Nevertheless, she was firm and resolute on her course, because of the pride that burnt within her.

So it was that, as the Sergeant presently came striding along on his homewards way, he was aware of Miss Anthea standing before him; whereupon he halted, removed his hat, and wished her good-afternoon.

"Sergeant," she said, "will you do something for me?"

"Anything you ask me, Miss Anthea, Ma'am—ever and always."

"I want you to take this letter to ... Mr. Cassilis, the Squire, will you?"

The Sergeant hesitated unwontedly, turning his hat about and about in his hand; finally he put it on, out of the way.

"Will you, Sergeant?"

"Since you ask me, Miss Anthea, Ma'am, I will."

"Give it into his own hand."

"Miss Anthea, Ma'am, I will."

Anthea walked on hastily, never looking behind, and so, coming back to the house, threw herself down by the open window, and stared out with unseeing eyes at the roses nodding their slumberous heads in the gentle breeze.

So the irrevocable step was taken. She had given her promise to marry Cassilis whenever he would, and she must abide by it.

Too late now for any hope of retreat; she had deliberately chosen her course and must follow it to the end.

"Begging your pardon, Miss Anthea, Mam..."

She started, glanced round, and saw Adam.

"Oh, you startled me, Adam... what is it?"

"Begging your pardon, Miss Anthea, but is it true as Mr. Belloo be gone away for good?"

"Yes, Adam."

"Why then, all I can say is as I'm sorry—ah! mortal sorry I be, an' my 'eart, Mam, my 'eart is likewise gloomy."

And then Adam told her he had made up the story of Bellew getting married—that he had agreed to say nothing to her, and the honest, well-meaning Adam touched his forehead with a square forefinger and trudged away.

But Anthea sat there, very still, with drooping head and vacant eyes.

And so it was done, the irrevocable step had been taken, she had given her promise, and now, having chosen her course, she must follow it to the end.

For, in Arcadia, it would seem that a promise is still a sacred thing.

Now, in a while, she lifted her eyes and encountered those of the smiling Cavalier above the mantel.

Then, as she looked, she stretched out her arms with a sudden yearning gesture.

"Oh!" she whispered. "If I were only . . . just a picture like you!"

Later that evening Anthea went and sat beneath "King Arthur" and felt very unhappy and alone, and even the beautiful sound of the blackbird seemed to mock her.

When he found her there, Small Porges said:

"Why, I do believe you're crying, Auntie Anthea! An' why are you here—all alone, an' by yourself?"

"I was listening to the blackbird, dear. I never heard him sing quite so . . . beautifully before."

"But blackbirds don't make people cry. An' I know you've been crying, 'cause you sound all quivery, you know."

"Do I, Georgy?"

"Yes. Is it 'cause you feel lonely?"

"Yes, dear."

"You've cried an awful lot lately, Auntie Anthea."

"Have I, dear?"

"Yes. An' it worried me, you know."

"I'm afraid I've been a great responsibility to you, Georgy dear," she said, with a rueful little laugh.

" 'Fraid you have; but I don't mind the 'sponsibility. I'll always take care of you, you know," said Small Porges, nodding.

He sat down so he could get his arm protectively about her, while Anthea stooped to kiss the top of his curly head.

"I promised my Uncle Porges I'd always take care of you; an' so I will."

"Yes, dear."

"Uncle Porges told me . . ."

"Never mind, dear. Don't let us talk of . . . him."

"Do you still hate him then, Auntie Anthea?"

"Hush, dear. It's very wrong to hate people."

"Yes, 'o course it is. Then perhaps if you don't hate him any more, perhaps you like him a bit—just a teeny bit, you know?"

"Why, there's the clock striking half-past eight, Georgy!"

"Yes, I hear it. But do you—the teeniest bit? Oh, can't you like him just a bit, for my sake, Auntie Anthea? I'm always trying to please you, an' I found you the fortune, you know.

"So now I want you to please me, an' tell me you like him—for my sake."

"But . . . Oh, Georgy dear! You don't understand."

"'Cause, you see," Small Porges continued, "after all, I found him for you, under a hedge, you know . . ."

"Ah, why did you, Georgy dear? We were so happy . . . before . . . he came . . ."

"But you couldn't have been, you know; you weren't married even then. So you couldn't have been really happy," said Small Porges, shaking his head.

"Why, Georgy, what do you mean?"

"Well, Uncle Porges told me that nobody can live happily ever after unless they're married first. So that was why I 'ranged for him to marry you, so you could both be happy, an' all revelry an' joy, like the fairy-tale, you know."

"But, you see, we aren't in a fairy-tale, dear; so I'm afraid we must make the best of things as they are."

She sighed again and rose.

"Come, Georgy; it's much later than I thought, and quite time you were in bed, dear."

"All right, Auntie Anthea. Only, don't you think it's just a bit cruel to send a boy to bed so very early, an' when the moon's so big, an' everything looks so frightfully fine. 'Sides . . ."

"Well, what now?" she asked a little wearily, as, obedient to his pleading gesture, she sat down again.

"Why, you haven't answered my question yet, you know."

"What question?" she said, not looking at him.

" 'Bout my Uncle Porges."

"But, Georgy . . . I . . ."

"You do like him, just a bit, don't you, please?"

Small Porges was standing before her as he waited for her answer; but now, seeing how she hesitated and avoided his eyes, he put one small hand beneath the dimple in her chin, so that she was forced to look at him.

"You do, please—don't you?"

Anthea hesitated. But, after all, he was gone, and nobody could hear, and Small Porges was so very small. And who could resist the entreaty in his big, wistful eyes?

Surely not Anthea. Therefore, with a sudden gesture of abandonment, she leant forward in his embrace, and rested her weary head against his small, manly shoulder.

"Yes," she whispered.

"Just as much as you like Mr. Cassilis?" he whispered back.

"Yes."

"A bit more, just a teeny bit more?"

"Yes."

"A lot more—lots an' lots—oceans more?"

"Yes."

The word was spoken, and, having uttered it, Anthea grew suddenly hot with shame, and mightily angry with herself, and would straightaway have given the world to have it unsaid.

The more so as she felt Small Porges' clasp tighten joyfully; and as she looked up, she fancied she read something like triumph in his eyes.

She drew away from him rather hastily and rose to her feet.

"Come," she said, speaking now in a vastly different tone. "It must be getting very late . . ."

"Yes. I 'specks it'll soon be nine o'clock now," he said, nodding.

"Then you ought to be in bed, fast asleep, instead of talking such nonsense out here. So come along at once, Sir."

"But, can't I stay up—just a little while? You see . . ."

"No."

"You see, it's such a magnif'cent night. It feels as though things might happen."

"Don't be so silly!"

"Well, but it does, you know."

"What do you mean? What things?"

"Well, it feels gnomy, to me. I 'specks there's lots of elves hidden about in the shadows, you know, an' peeping at us."

"There aren't any elves or gnomes," said Anthea petulantly, for she was still furiously angry with herself.

"But my Uncle Porges told me . . ."

"Oh!" cried Anthea, stamping her foot suddenly. "Can't you talk of anyone, or anything ... but ... him? I'm tired to death of him and his very name!"

"But I thought you liked him an awful lot —an' ..."

"Well, I don't."

"But you said ..."

"Never mind what I said; it's time you were in bed asleep. So come along at once, Sir!"

So they went on through the orchard together, very silently, for Small Porges was inclined to be indignant, but much more inclined to be hurt.

Thus, they had not gone so very far when he spoke, in a voice that he would have described as quivery.

"Don't you think that you're just the teeniest bit cruel to me, Auntie Anthea?" he enquired wistfully. "After I prayed an' prayed till I found a fortune for you? Don't you, please?"

Surely Anthea was a woman of moods tonight. For, even while he spoke, she stopped and turned and fell on her knees, and caught him in her arms, kissing him many times.

"Yes, yes, dear! I'm hateful to you, horrid to you. But I don't mean to be. There, forgive me!"

"Oh, it's all right again now, Auntie Anthea, thank you. I only thought you were just a bit hard, you know, 'cause it is such a magnif'cent night, isn't it?"

"Yes, dear; and perhaps there are gnomes and pixies about. Anyhow, we can pretend there are, if you like, as we used to ..."

"Oh, will you? That would be fine. Then,

please may I go with you as far as the brook? We'll wander, you know. I've never wandered with you in the moonlight, an' I do love to hear the brook talking to itself. So will you wander— just this once?"

"Well," said Anthea, hesitating, "it's very late."

"Nearly nine o'clock, yes; but oh, please don't forget that I found a fortune for you."

"Very well," she said, smiling. "Just this once."

Now, as they went together, hand in hand, through the moonlight, Small Porges talked fast, and very much at random, while his eyes, bright and eager, glanced expectantly towards every patch of shadow, doubtless in search of gnomes and pixies.

But Anthea saw nothing of this, and heard nothing of the suppressed excitement of his voice, for she was thinking that by now Mr. Cassilis had read her letter, and that he might even now be on his way to Dapplemere.

She even fancied once or twice that she could hear the gallop of his horse's hoofs, and when he came he would want to kiss her!

"Why do you shiver so, Auntie Anthea? Are you cold?"

"No, dear."

"Well then, why are you so quiet to me? I've asked you a question—three times."

"Have you, dear? I was thinking. What was the question?"

"I was asking you if you would be awful frightened s'posing we did find a pixie, or a gnome, in the shadows. An' would you be so very awfully frightened if a gnome—a great big one, you know—came jumping out an' ran off with you? Would you?"

"No," said Anthea, with another quiver. "No, dear. I think I should be . . . rather glad of it."

"Should you, Auntie? I'm so awful glad you wouldn't be frightened. O' course, I don't s'pose there are gnomes—I mean great big ones really, you know; but there might be, on a magnif'cent night like this. If you shiver again, Auntie Anthea, you'll have to take my coat."

"I thought I heard a horse galloping. Hush!"

They had reached the stile by now—the stile with the crooked, lurking nail—and she leant there awhile to listen.

"I'm sure I heard something, away there, on the road."

"I didn't," Small Porges replied stoutly. "So, take my hand, please, an' let me 'sist you over the stile."

So they crossed the stile and presently came to the brook. It seemed to Anthea that it was laughing at her, mocking and taunting her with the future. And now, amidst the laughter, were sobs and tearful murmurs; and now, again, it seemed to be the prophetic voice of old Nannie.

"By force ye shall be wooed, and by force ye shall be wed; and there is no man strong enough to do it, but him as he bears the Tiger Mark upon him."

The Tiger Mark!

Alas, how very far from the truth were poor old Nannie's dreams, after all. The dreams which Anthea had very nearly believed in, once or twice! How foolish it had all been; and yet, even now . . .

Anthea had been leaning over the gurgling waters while all this passed through her mind.

But now she started at the sound of a heavy footfall on the planking of the bridge behind her, and in that same instant she was encircled by a powerful arm, caught up in a strong embrace, swung from her feet, and borne away through the shadows of the little copse.

It was very dark in the wood, but she knew instinctively whose arms these were that held her so close and carried her so easily. Away, through the shadows of the wood, away from the haunting dread of the future, from which there had seemed no chance or hope of escape.

And, knowing all this, she made no struggle and uttered no word.

And now the trees thinned out, and from under her lashes she saw the face above her; the thick, black brows drawn together, the close set of the lips, the grim prominence of the strong, square chin.

And now they were in the road, and now he had lifted her into an automobile, had sprung in beside her, and they were off, gliding swift and ever swifter under the shadows of the trees.

Still neither spoke, nor looked at each other, only she leant away from him against the cushions, while he kept his frowning eyes fixed upon the road ahead.

But at last, finding him so silent and impassive, she stole a look at him beneath her lashes.

He wore no hat, and as she looked at him with his yellow hair, his length of limb, and his massive shoulders, he might have been a fierce Viking, and she, his captive, taken by strength of arm, borne away by force—by force.

And, hereupon, as the car hummed over the smooth road, it seemed to find a voice—a subtle, mocking voice, very like the voice of the brook that had murmured to her over and over again.

"By force ye shall be wooed, and by force ye shall be wed."

The very trees whispered it as they passed, and her heart throbbed in time to it.

"By force ye shall be wooed, and by force ye shall be wed."

So she leant as far from him as she might, watching him with frightened eyes, while he frowned upon the road in front, and the car rocked and swayed with their going, as they whirled onward through moonlight and through shadow, faster and faster.

Yet not so fast as the beating of her heart, wherein was fear, and shame, and anger, and another feeling—but greatest of all now was fear. Could this be the placid, soft-spoken gentleman she had known?

This man with the implacable eyes, and brutal jaw, who neither spoke to nor looked at her, and frowned always at the road before him?

And so the fear grew within her, fear of the man whom she knew, and knew not at all. She clasped her hands nervously together, watching him with dilating eyes as the car slowed down, for the road made a sudden turn hereabouts.

And still he neither looked at her nor spoke to her, and therefore, because she could bear the silence no longer, she spoke in a voice that sounded strangely faint, and far-away, and that shook and trembled in spite of her.

"Where are you . . . taking me?"

"To be married," he answered, never looking at her.

"You wouldn't . . . dare."

"Wait and see," he said with a nod.

"Oh! But what do . . . you mean?"

The fear in her voice was more manifest than ever.

"I mean that you are mine, you always were, you always must, and always shall be. So I'm going to marry you, in about half-an-hour, by Special Licence."

Still he did not even glance towards her, and she looked away over the countryside, lonely and desolate under the moon.

"I want you, you see," he went on. "I want you more than I ever wanted anything in the world. I need you, because without you my life will be utterly purposeless, and empty.

"So I have taken you because you are mine. I know it—ah, yes, and deep down in your woman's heart you know it too. And so I am going to marry you, yes, I am, unless . . ."

And here he brought the car to a standstill, and, turning, looked at her for the first time.

Before the look in his eyes, her own wavered, and fell, lest he should read within them that which she would hide from him, and which she knew they must reveal.

That which was neither shame nor anger, nor fear; but the "other feeling" for which she dared find no name. And thus, for a long moment, there was silence.

At last she spoke, though with her eyes still hidden.

"Unless?" she repeated breathlessly.

"Anthea, look at me!"

But Anthea only stooped her head the lower, so he leant forward and, even as Small Porges had done, set his hand beneath the dimple in her chin, and lifted her proud, unwilling face.

"Anthea, look at me!"

And now what could Anthea do but obey?

"Unless," he said, as her glance at last met his, "unless you can tell me now, as your eyes look into mine—that you love Cassilis. Tell me that, and I will take you back this very instant, and never trouble you again; but, unless you do tell me that, why then, your pride shall not blast two lives, if I can help it.

"Now speak!"

But Anthea was silent. Also, she would have turned aside from his searching look, but his arm was about her, strong and compelling.

So needs must she suffer him to look down into her very heart, for it seemed to her that in that moment he had rent away every stitch and shred of Pride's enfolding mantle, and that he saw the truth at last.

But if he did he gave no sign; he only turned and set the car humming upon its way once more.

On they went through the midsummer night. Up hill and down hill, by cross-road and by-lane, until as they climbed a long ascent they saw a tall figure standing upon the top of the hill, in the attitude of one who waits; and who, spying them, immediately raised a very stiff arm, whereupon this figure was joined by another.

Now, as the car drew near, Anthea, with a thrill of pleasure, recognised the Sergeant, standing very much as though he were on parade, and with honest-faced Peterday beside him, who stumped joyfully forward and, with a bob of his head and a scrape of his wooden leg, held out his hand to her.

Like one in a dream she took the sailor's hand to step from the car, and like one in a dream she walked on between the soldier and the sailor, who now reached out to her, each, a hand equally big and equally gentle, to aid her up certain crumbling and time-worn steps.

On they went together, until they came to a place of whispering echoes, where lights burnt, few and dim.

And here, still as one in a dream, she spoke those words which gave her life, henceforth, into the keeping of him who stood beside her, whose strong hand trembled as he set upon her finger that which is an emblem of eternity.

Like one in a dream she took the pen and signed her name obediently, where they directed. And yet could this really be herself, this silent, submissive creature?

And now they were out upon the moonlit road again, seated in the car, while Peterday, his hat in his hand, was speaking to her—and yet was it to her?

"Mrs. Belloo, Ma'am," he was saying, "on this here monumentous occasion . . ."

" 'Monumentous' is the only word for it, Peterday," added the Sergeant.

"On this here monumentous occasion, Mrs. Belloo," the sailor proceeded, "my shipmate Dick and myself, Ma'am, respectfully beg the favour of saluting the bride. Mrs. Belloo, by your leave, here's health and happiness, Ma'am."

And hereupon the old sailor kissed her, right heartily, then made way for the Sergeant, who, after a moment's hesitation, followed suit.

"A fair wind and prosperous," cried Peterday, flourishing his hat.

"And God bless you both," said the Sergeant, as the car shot away.

So it was done—the irrevocable step had been taken!

Her life and future had passed forever into the keeping of him who sat so silent beside her, who neither spoke nor looked at her, but frowned ever at the road before him.

On sped the car, faster and faster. Yet not so fast as the beating of her heart, wherein was still something of fear and shame.

But the greatest of all was that other emotion, and the name of it was Joy.

Now, presently, the car slowed down, and he spoke to her, though without turning his head. And yet something in his voice thrilled through her strangely.

"Look, Anthea, the moon is at the full to-night."

"Yes," she answered.

"'And happiness shall come riding astride the full moon,'" he quoted. "Old Nannie is rather a wonderful old witch, after all, isn't she?"

"Yes."

"And then there is our nephew, my dear little Porges. But for him, Happiness would have been a stranger to me all the days, Anthea. He dreamed that the Money Moon spoke to him, and—but he shall tell you of that for himself."

Anthea noticed that he spoke without once looking towards her. Indeed, it seemed that he avoided glancing towards her, of set design and purpose; and his deep voice quivered now and then in a way she had never heard before.

Therefore, her heart throbbed the faster, and she kept her gaze bent downwards, and thus, chancing to see the shimmer of that which was upon her finger, she blushed, and hid it in the fold of her gown.

"Anthea."

"Yes?"

"You have no regrets, have you?"

"No," she whispered.

"We shall soon be home now."

"Yes."

"And you are mine forever and always, Anthea! You aren't—afraid of me any more, are you?"

"No."

"Nor ever will be?"

"Nor . . . ever will be."

Now, as the car swept round the bend, behold, yet two other figures standing beside the way.

"Yo ho! Captain!" cried a voice. "Oh please —heave to, Uncle Porges?"

And Small Porges came running forward to meet them. Yet, remembering Miss Priscilla tapping along behind him, he turned back to give her his hand, like the kindly, small gentleman that he was.

And now Miss Priscilla had Anthea in her arms, and they were kissing each other and murmuring over each other, as loving women will, while Small Porges stared at the car, and all things pertaining thereto, more especially the glaring head-lights, with great, wondering eyes.

At length, having seen Anthea and Miss Priscilla safely stowed, he clambered up beside Bellew and gave him the word to proceed.

What pen can describe his ecstatic delight as he sat there with one hand hooked into the pocket of Uncle Porges' coat, and with the cool night wind whistling through his curls.

So great was it that Bellew was constrained to turn aside and make a wide detour purely for the sake of the radiant joy in Small Porges' eager face.

When at last they came in sight of Dapplemere, and the great machine crept up the rutted, grassy lane, Small Porges sighed and spoke.

"Auntie Anthea," he said, "are you sure that you are married—nice an' tight, you know?"

"Yes, dear," she answered. "Why . . . yes, Georgy."

"But you don't look a bit different, you know, either of you. Are you quite—quite sure? 'Cause I shouldn't like you to disappoint me after all."

"Never fear, my Porges," said Bellew. "I made quite sure of it, while I had the chance—look!"

As he spoke, he took Anthea's left hand and drew it out into the moonlight, so that Small Porges could see the shining ring upon her finger.

"Oh," he said, nodding his head. "Then that makes it all right, I s'pose; an' you aren't angry with me 'cause I let a great big gnome come an' carry you off, are you, Auntie Anthea?"

"No, dear."

"Why then, everything's quite magnif'cent, isn't it? An' now we are going to live happily ever after, all of us.

"An' Uncle Porges is going to take us to sail the oceans in his ship—he's got a ship that all belongs to his very own self, you know, Auntie Anthea. So all will be revelry an' joy—just like the fairy-tale, after all!"

At last they came to the door of the ancient house of Dapplemere. Whereupon, very suddenly, Adam appeared, bare-armed, from the stables, and looked from Bellew's radiant face to Miss Anthea's shy eyes, threw back his head, vented his great laugh, and was immediately solemn again.

"Miss Anthea," he said, wringing and twisting his hat, "or, I think I should say—Mrs. Belloo, Mam, there ain't no word for it—leastways, not as I knows of, nohow. No words be strong enough to tell the joy, Mam, as fills us—one an' all!"

Here he waved his hand to where stood the comely Prudence, with the two rosy-cheeked maids peeping over her buxom shoulders.

"Only," pursued Adam, "I be glad—oh, mortal glad, I be—as 'tis you, Mr. Belloo, Sir. There ain't a man in all the world—or, as you might say, universe—as is so proper as you to be the husband of our Miss Anthea—as was—not nohow, Mr. Belloo, Sir. I wish you joy—a joy as shall grow wi' the years, and abide wi' you always—both of ye."

"That is a very excellent thought, Adam," said Bellew. "And I think I should like to shake hands on it."

"An' now, Mrs. Belloo, Mam," Adam concluded, "wi' your kind permission, I'll step into the kitchen an' drink a glass o' Prue's ale—to your 'ealth and 'appiness. If I stay here any longer, I won't say but what I shall burst out a-singing in your very face, Mam, for I do be that 'appy-'earted. Lord!"

With which exclamation, Adam laughed again, and, turning about, strode away to the kitchen, with Prudence and the rosy-cheeked maids, laughing as he went.

"Oh, my dears," said little Miss Priscilla, "I've hoped for this—prayed for it; because I believe he is worthy of you, Anthea, and because you have both loved each other from the very beginning; oh, you have!

"And so, my dears, your happiness is my happiness, and . . . Oh, goodness me! Here I stand talking sentimental nonsense while our Small Porges is simply dropping asleep as he stands!"

"'Fraid I'm a bit tired," Small Porges admitted; "but it's been a magnif'cent night. An' I think, Uncle Porges, when we sail away in your ship, I think I'd like to sail round the Horn first, 'cause they say it's always blowing, you know, and I should love to hear it blow. An' now—good-night!"

"Wait a minute, my Porges. Just tell us what it was that the Money Moon said to you last night. Will you?"

"Well," said Small Porges, shaking his head, and smiling a slow, sly smile, "I don't s'pose we'd better talk about it, Uncle Porges, 'cause you see, it was such a very great secret; an' 'sides—I'm awful sleepy, you know."

He nodded slumberously, kissed Anthea sleepily, and, giving Miss Priscilla his hand, went drowsily into the house.

But, as for Bellew, it seemed to him that this was the hour for which he had lived all his life, and though he spoke nothing of this thought, yet Anthea knew it instinctively.

She knew, too, why he had avoided looking

at her hitherto, and what had caused the tremor in his voice, despite his iron self-control.

And therefore, now that they were alone, she spoke hurriedly and at random.

"What did he . . . Georgy, mean by . . . your ship?"

"Why, I promised to take him on a cruise in the yacht, if you cared to come, Anthea?"

"Yacht," she repeated. "Are you so dreadfully rich?"

"I'm afraid we are." He nodded. "But at least it has the advantage of being better than if we were dreadfully poor, hasn't it?"

Now, in the midst of the garden, there was an old sun-dial, worn by time; and it chanced that they came and leant there, side by side, and, looking down upon the dial, Bellew saw certain characters graven there, in the form of a posey.

"What does it say here, Anthea?" he asked.

But Anthea shook her head.

"That you must read for yourself," she said, not looking at him.

So he took her hand in his, and with her slender finger spelled out this motto:

Time and youths do flee awaie,
Love, Oh! Love then, whiles ye may.

"Anthea," he said, and again she heard the tremor in his voice, "you have been my wife nearly three-quarters of an hour, and in all that time I haven't dared to look at you, because, if I had, I must have kissed you, and I meant to wait—until your own good time. But you have not yet told me that you love me, Anthea."

She did not speak or move; indeed, she was

so very still that he had to bend down to see her face.

Then, all at once, her lashes were raised, and her eyes looked up into his, deep and dark, with a passionate tenderness.

"Aunt Priscilla was quite right," she said, speaking in her low, sweet, thrilling voice. "I have loved you . . . from the very beginning . . . I think!"

And with a soft, murmurous sigh, she lifted her lips to his.

ABOUT THE EDITOR

BARBARA CARTLAND, the world's most famous romantic novelist, who is also an historian, playwright, lecturer, political speaker and television personality, has now written over 200 books.

She has also had many historical works published and has written four autobiographies as well as the biographies of her mother and that of her brother Ronald Cartland, who was the first Member of Parliament to be killed in the last war. This book has a preface by Sir Winston Churchill.

Barbara Cartland has sold 100 million books over the world, more than half of these in the U.S.A. She broke the world record in 1975 by writing twenty books, and her own record in 1976 with twenty-one. In addition, her album of love songs has just been published, sung with the Royal Philharmonic Orchestra.

In private life, Barbara Cartland, who is a Dame of the Order of St. John of Jerusalem, has fought for better conditions and salaries for Midwives and Nurses. As President of the Royal College of Midwives (Hertfordshire Branch), she has been invested with the first Badge of Office ever given in Great Britain, which was subscribed to by the Midwives themselves. She has also championed the cause for old people and founded the first Romany Gypsy Camp in the world.

Barbara Cartland is deeply interested in Vitamin Therapy and is President of the British National Association for Health.

BARBARA CARTLAND
PRESENTS
THE ANCIENT WISDOM SERIES

The world's all-time bestselling author of romantic fiction, Barbara Cartland, has established herself as High Priestess of Love in its purest and most traditionally romantic form.

"We have," she says, "in the last few years thrown out the spiritual aspect of love and concentrated only on the crudest and most debased sexual side.

"Love at its highest has inspired mankind since the beginning of time. Civilization's greatest pictures, music, prose and poetry have all been written under the influence of love. This love is what we all seek despite the temptations of the sensuous, the erotic, the violent and the perversions of pornography.

"I believe that for the young and the idealistic, my novels with their pure heroines and high ideals are a guide to happiness. Only by seeking the Divine Spark which exists in every human being, can we create a future built on the foundation of faith."

Barbara Cartland is also well known for her Library of Love, classic tales of romance, written by famous authors like Elinor Glyn and Ethel M. Dell, which have been personally selected and specially adapted for today's readers by Miss Cartland.

"These novels I have selected and edited for my 'Library of Love' are all stories with which the readers can identify themselves and also be assured that right will triumph in the end. These tales elevate and activate the mind rather than debase it as so many modern stories do."

Now, in August, Bantam presents the first four novels in a new Barbara Cartland Ancient Wisdom series. The books are THE FORBIDDEN CITY by Barbara Cartland, herself; THE ROMANCE OF TWO WORLDS by Marie Corelli; THE HOUSE OF FULFILLMENT by L. Adams Beck; and BLACK LIGHT by Talbot Mundy.

"Now I am introducing something which I think is of vital importance at this moment in history. Following my own autobiographical book I SEEK THE MIRACULOUS, which Dutton is publishing in hardcover this summer, I am offering those who seek 'the world behind the world' novels which contain, besides a fascinating story, the teaching of Ancient Wisdom.

"In the snow-covered vastnesses of the Himalayas, there are lamaseries filled with manuscripts which have been kept secret for century upon century. In the depths of the tropical jungles and the arid wastes of the deserts, there are also those who know the esoteric mysteries which few can understand.

"Yet some of their precious and sacred knowledge has been revealed to writers in the past. These books I have collected, edited and offer them to those who want to look beyond this greedy, grasping, materialistic world to find their own souls.

"I believe that Love, human and divine, is the jail-breaker of that prison of selfhood which confines and confuses us . . .

"I believe that for those who have attained enlightenment, super-normal (not super-human) powers are available to those who seek them."

All Barbara Cartland's own novels and her Library of Love are available in Bantam Books, wherever paperbacks are sold. Look for her Ancient Wisdom Series to be available in August.

Barbara Cartland

The world's bestselling author of romantic fiction. Her stories are always captivating tales of intrigue, adventure and love.

☐ 11372	LOVE AND THE LOATHSOME LEOPARD		$1.50
☐ 11410	THE NAKED BATTLE		$1.50
☐ 11512	THE HELL-CAT AND THE KING		$1.50
☐ 11537	NO ESCAPE FROM LOVE		$1.50
☐ 11580	THE CASTLE MADE FOR LOVE		$1.50
☐ 11579	THE SIGN OF LOVE		$1.50
☐ 11595	THE SAINT AND THE SINNER		$1.50
☐ 11649	A FUGITIVE FROM LOVE		$1.50
☐ 11797	THE TWISTS AND TURNS OF LOVE		$1.50
☐ 11801	THE PROBLEMS OF LOVE		$1.50
☐ 11751	LOVE LEAVES AT MIDNIGHT		$1.50
☐ 11882	MAGIC OR MIRAGE		$1.50
☐ 10712	LOVE LOCKED IN		$1.50
☐ 11959	LORD RAVENSCAR'S REVENGE		$1.50
☐ 11488	THE WILD, UNWILLING WIFE		$1.50
☐ 11555	LOVE, LORDS, AND LADY-BIRDS		$1.50

Buy them at your local bookstore or use this handy coupon: